Billionaire Grump

Misha Bell

♠ Mozaika Publications ♠

Published by Mozaika Publications, an imprint of Mozaika LLC.
www.mozaikallc.com

Cover by Najla Qamber Designs
www.najlaqamberdesigns.com

ISBN: 978-1-63142-784-8
Paperback ISBN: 978-1-63142-787-9

Chapter 1

Lucius

THE LOBBY IS TEAMING with cacophonous meatsacks, and I'm late.

I readjust my giant headphones and up the volume until the sound of heavy metal drowns out the infuriating voices.

Yeah. That's a little better, though what I really need is a pair of glasses that can use Augmented Reality to filter out the people. Alas, such glasses do not exist yet.

Oh, well. Such is life—or *sic vita est* as the Romans would've said.

Pretending I'm alone, I stride past the security desk. The guards know better than to check my ID. After all, I own the company that owns the building.

When I'm halfway to my elevator, I begin to have hope that I'll make the meeting. Thanks to my reputation, everyone steps aside and makes way for me.

Wait. Spoke too soon.

A man stands in my path. A man whose name I don't recall, but I'm pretty sure he's a VP of something dumb, like marketing.

Does he not realize how late I am for the Novus Rome meeting? Everyone knows it's my highest priority at the moment and is thus sacrosanct.

The man doesn't seem to have a clue. He's clearly not high enough on the corporate ladder to be needed for the meeting. Or he *is* high, but in the other sense of the word.

Mindbogglingly, his lips are moving.

As in, he's talking to me.

I give him the IANE, my patented "I am not entertained" glare.

His lips are still moving.

Bullshit like this is why my dream is to replace all my employees with robots. I'd give a billion dollars to do that, or a couple years of my life. And maybe even my Russell Crowe-signed *Gladiator* poster.

I pull away the right earcup. "What?"

"Hello, sir. I just wanted to tell you that our last campaign went outstandingly well and—"

I tune out the rest. I can always tell what people are really saying, and in this case, it is: *Promote me. Please promote me. I know I don't deserve it, but pretty please promote me.*

The irony is, he has just hurt his chances for that

promotion with his rudeness. That is, if I recall his name come the end of the year...

I place the earcup back in its place. "Excuse me, I'm late."

Ignoring his stammered apologies, I stride purposefully to the elevator, and this time, my expression is such that no other meatsack dares interrupt me.

As I walk, my stomach rumbles.

Damn it. I should've eaten something.

My stomach growls in agreement.

I hate this and anything that reminds me that I'm a slave to biology. As soon as I can upload my brain into a robot body, I'm doing it and never looking back—but for now, I hope there are snacks at the meeting.

Reaching my elevator, I check the clock on my phone as I wait for the doors to crawl open.

I'm a minute late. Hopefully, Eidith can smooth things out with the real estate guy—whatever his name is. Actually, given how much I want this particular plot of land, I should really try to remember his name.

I pull up my calendar, open the meeting invite, and repeat the stupid-sounding last name over and over in my head.

Yep. Got it now. I step into my elevator and press the top button: LXXXVIII.

My phone rings.

I frown at it, until I realize it's Gram calling. Accepting the call, I jab at the "door open" button to make sure the elevator doesn't close. My grandmother is the only person whose calls I always take, and I don't want to lose reception and thus needlessly worry her.

"Lucius, pumpkin, how are you doing this beautiful morning?" she asks, and I can picture her dimpled smile on the other end of the line.

"Hungry and late," I say, not doing a good job of avoiding another accusation of sounding like the Grinch.

"I keep telling you, and you don't listen: you need a good woman to take care of you."

Sure. I'll add "find good woman" to my to-do list, right after "get a hole in the head."

"How's your back?" I ask in lieu of a reply.

Gram pulled a muscle while opening a jar of peach jam the other week, which prompted me to fire her home attendant and replace her with a burly bodyguard. His job involves opening all future jars in Gram's house in addition to looking after her.

"Oh, much better." With a chuckle, she adds, "Turns out Aleksy was a masseuse back in Poland."

I take a thoughtful sip from my water bottle as I process what I've just heard. The bodyguard got handsy with my grandmother? Do I need to fire him or raise his salary?

"Wait, didn't you say you were late?" Gram asks.

"A little. No big deal."

"Go," she says. "Call me after."

"Will do."

She hangs up, and I smash the "door close" button.

4

The doors slowly slide closed—way, way too slowly. This is what you get when you opt for looks over function. The doors are in the Roman style I prefer, but all the adornments make them move slower than a turtle that's been bitten by a radioactive snail.

Then, when only a tiny opening remains, a dainty, sandal-clad foot with sparkly pink nail polish wedges itself between the doors.

A foot that's close to perfect—so much so, it serves as another unwelcome reminder of my biology.

The person the foot belongs to is brave. Had this door been designed with efficiency in mind, this maneuver would've severed the foot, and the elevator would've gone on its way as if nothing had happened. Alas, the engineer I hired was clearly a tree-hugging vegan because the elevator doors open back up, just as slowly as they closed.

I glare at my watch again.

Five minutes late now.

Motherfucking fuck.

I turn my attention back to the foot and prepare to rip into its owner.

Chapter 2

Juno

I STEP into the building and pause my audiobook —*Insignificant Events in the Life of a Cactus*. So far, the book is great, but to my disappointment, it's about a human girl and not a cactus as the title would imply.

As I take in the lobby, my eyes grow wide. The place looks modern on the outside, but it's like an Ancient Roman museum on the inside.

I readjust my dress—not that it will help me blend in. The suits I see around here likely cost more than I make in a year. Worse yet, the chilly air roughens the skin on my arms, making me realize that my outfit, a yellow summer dress I got on sale at TJMaxx, is a failure on a practical level as well, as it's doing a poor job of protecting me from the overzealous AC. My sandals aren't helping either.

Then I spot something nearby that makes me feel warm... at least on the inside.

It's a wall covered in greenery. There are vines, moss, and ferns, which are all great, but there's also representation from my favorite living thing in the whole world: the cactus.

Unable to stop myself, I walk over to the wall, where I come face to adorable spines with a Haworthia retusa, a.k.a. a star cactus.

"Hi, little cactusie. You're a real star, aren't you?" I croon in a soft whisper. Most people don't understand when I talk to plants in front of them. In fact, they often refer me to a psychiatrist. I lower my voice further. "Are you thirsty? Hungry? Cold?"

At home, I know my pet cactus El Duderino so well I can picture (and say out loud) what his reply would be if we lived in a better universe, one where cactuses *could* talk. I wouldn't dare reply as this little hottie, though, even if we were better acquainted, because that's something even fewer witnesses would understand. Instead, I make sure no one is looking, and then I stick my index finger into the soil next to the gorgeous creature.

Yep. The soil feels just right—not too wet. Of course, if I get this job, I'll bring my trusty tensiometer to be sure.

By saguaro spines, I almost forgot about the job, or more specifically, the interview that will start in a few minutes.

How could I be so scatterbrained? This is not my typical small-business client. This building belongs to a corporation—which means if I get the gig, I'll finally make the money I need to pay for my college tuition.

Adrenaline spiking, I hurry over to the security desk—and nearly bump into a man wearing huge headphones.

Damn. He's not even bothering to look at whom he might trample. Then again, if a man *was* going to ram me, this one might not be a bad specimen for the job. He's tall, broad-shouldered, with angular, brooding features, a Roman nose, and intelligent eyes the color of steel. He has thick, bushy eyebrows, and his dark hair is cut in a spiky fauxhawk Caesar that makes me want to run my fingers through it. Speaking of hair, I wonder if his stubble would feel scratchy on my thigh if he—

Snap out of it, Juno.

Interview.

A few feet away, the stranger is stopped by some suit. His reaction isn't pretty. He very nearly growls at the suit.

What a grouch. Is this what I'm going to have to put up with now that I'm going corporate? At least my interview is with a woman, so definitely not *this* character. I'm not sure how long I could put up with him before snarking back. Not to mention, his looks would be distracting during an interview.

With effort, I tear my gaze away from the annoyingly attractive stranger. I have to focus on getting the job.

Sprinting to the security desk, I hand over my driver's license to the guy there, explaining that I'm here to interview for the plant caretaker position.

The guard checks my ID and smirks. "Juno, huh? Did your parents name you after that movie?"

If I had a cactus for every time someone made that excuse for a joke, I'd be able to give the Mojave Desert a run for its money.

I smile prettily at him. "You mean the movie that came out in 2007? If that's your way of saying I look like a teenager, I'll take it as a compliment."

He looks back at my ID and whistles. "You're thirty? I would've guessed much younger."

Someone's on a roll. That's the second most common thing I hear, thanks to my height impairment and the cherubic cheeks I've yet to grow out of. If he tells me I look wholesome and virginal, we'll hit the evil trifecta. Or is it that a quadfecta?

Hiding my thoughts behind a megawatt smile, I bat my eyelashes at him. "Thank you. You're sweet." Like anti-freeze.

"No problem." He extends a visitor's pass my way, but then he pulls it out of my reach at the last second—something I'd hate even if it weren't for my height. "You don't have any weapons on you, right?"

I shake my head vehemently and paste on my most innocent smile. As it so happens, I kind of do: in my purse is a cat named Atonic, who is lethal—at least for the few minutes of the day when she isn't catatonic.

Yes, I know. I'm bringing a live animal to an important interview. I figure I should be safe, though, as there's a 99.999 percent chance that the cat will sleep through the whole thing. I'm cat-sitting for Pearl, my bestie who failed to inform me that her fur child turns into a beast when left alone. If my dear El Duderino weren't a cactus, he would've already met the giant saguaro in the sky-desert of cactus heaven. Thankfully, though, it's my furniture that's taken the brunt of the razor-sharp claws thus far.

"Great." The guard finally proffers the pass again, and it takes a lot of willpower to gently take it instead of rudely snatching it away.

Should I ask him where I can find the bathroom?

Nah. He seems like the type to make a "pissed off" joke, and I don't think I could continue being polite if he did. I'll just have to make sure to locate a bathroom as soon as I get upstairs.

Thanking the guard, I head over to the nearby turnstile and swipe the pass through the reader.

A green light informs me that I can proceed. I step through, only to realize I forgot to ask the guard which elevator bank to take to get to the forty-eighth floor.

With dread, I scan my surroundings. Thanks to my dyslexia, simple tasks like this are stressful. Numbers are particularly tricky for me to read. If I see a phone number without the area code in parenthesis and a dash after the first three digits, my brain wants to melt.

Whew.

There are only two elevator banks, and I can easily parse the numbers that explain where to go. I think. I'm pretty sure the bank on the left is for floors one to twenty-nine, while the other services the rest of the building—including floor forty-eight.

As I head over there, I see the nearest elevator close shut. Then another. And one more.

Ugh. Of course they all left without me. The likelihood of things going wrong must be directly proportional to how badly I want to get my degree and therefore this job.

Wait. I spot the doors of the farthest elevator only beginning to close.

This is my chance.

I sprint for all I'm worth and make it just in time to stick my foot in to prevent the doors from fully closing.

Hmm.

These doors look different from the others. Weird. The important thing is that they actually notice my foot and open up. The alternative would've been to lose my foot, and I'm attached to it.

As the elevator reopens, I see a man inside.

The grumpy hottie from earlier.

Oh, boy.

If glares could kill, I'd be a corpse eaten by a vulture and excreted as guano to serve as fertilizer for an industrious cactus.

Chapter 3

Lucius

THE DOORS OPEN, and I see to whom the pretty foot is attached: a petite woman. Before I can rip into her for daring to use my elevator, she flutters over to the wall with the elevator buttons. She moves too quickly for me to get a good look, but I can see her reflection in a mirrored wall.

Unable to help myself, I stare at it. Even though this woman has delayed me, I find myself curious about her—stupid biology at work once more. In my biology's defense, this stranger epitomizes the Ancient Roman standards of female beauty. Soft and curvy, with wide hips, small breasts, wheat-colored hair, and large, almond-shaped eyes the shade of honey, she reminds me of some of the statues at my villa. Hell, she's even as short as the average woman of that time.

Speaking of her stature, it makes it hard to tell how old she is. Based on her reckless behavior, I bet she's in her early twenties—as in, before brain development is complete.

Why is she staring at the elevator buttons so intently?

Also, is she muttering something?

Morbidly curious, I pause my music and turn off the noise cancellation function on my headphones.

"What kind of an idiot would use Roman numerals for this?" I hear her mumble. "And why are they not in neat rows like all other elevator buttons?"

I clench my jaw.

That "idiot" would be me. I love Roman numerals, and everyone knows this is *my* elevator. As to the lack of rows, that was the engineer's idea.

Hesitantly, she presses the button labeled XLIV.

We stop instantly.

She sticks her head out of the elevator, curses under her breath, and presses XLVI.

Again, this seems not to be the floor she needs, so she presses XLIX, then LVIII.

After two more stops, I take my headphones off. "Are you five?" I growl.

She turns on me. "What?"

"You're pressing all the buttons," I say icily. "Like a child."

And as I watch in reluctant fascination, her round cheeks turn red and her nostrils flare.

Chapter 4

Juno

"ARE YOU CALLING ME STUPID?" I snap. Anyone could have trouble with these damn buttons, not just a person with dyslexia.

He looks pointedly at the buttons. "Stupid is as stupid does."

I grind my teeth, painfully. "You're an asshole. And you've watched *Forrest Gump* one too many times."

His lips flatten. "That movie wasn't the origin of that saying. It's from Latin: *Stultus est sicut stultus facit*."

I roll my eyes. "What kind of pretentious *stultus* quotes Latin?"

The steel in his eyes is so cold I bet my tongue would get stuck if I tried to lick his eyeball. "I don't know. Maybe the 'idiot' who happens to like everything related to Rome, including their numerals."

My jaw drops open. "You made this decision?" I wave toward the elevator buttons.

He nods.

Shit. He probably heard me earlier, which means I started the insults. In my defense, he did make an idiotic choice.

I exhale a frustrated breath. "If you're such an expert on Roman numerals, you could've told me which one to press."

He crosses his arms over his chest. "You didn't ask me."

My hackles rise again. "Ask you? You looked like you might bite my head off for just existing."

"That's because you delayed—"

The elevator jerks to a stop, and the lights around us dim.

We both stare at the doors.

They stay shut.

He turns to me and narrows his eyes accusingly. "What did you press now?"

"Me? How? I've been facing you. Unfortunately."

With an annoying headshake, he stalks toward the panel with the buttons, and I have to leap away before I get trampled.

"You probably pressed something earlier," he mutters. "Why else would we be stuck?"

Why is it illegal to choke people? Just a few seconds with my hands on his throat would be a calming exercise.

Instead, I glare at his back, which is blocking my view of what he's doing, if anything. "The poor elevator probably just committed suicide over these Roman numerals. It knew that when someone sees things like L and XL, they think of T-shirt sizes for Neanderthal types like you. And don't get me started on that XXX button, which is a clear reference to porn. It creates a hostile work env—"

"Can you shut up so I can get us out of this?" he snaps.

His words bring home the reality of our situation: it's been over a minute, and the doors are still closed.

Dear saguaro, am I really stuck here? With this guy? What about my interview?

"Silence, finally," he says with satisfaction and moves to the side, so I see him jam his finger at the "help" button.

"It's a miracle that's not in Latin," I can't help but say. "Or Klingon."

"Hello?" he says into the speaker under the button, his voice dripping with irritation.

No reply, not even static.

"Anyone there?" His annoyance is clearly rising to new heights. "I'm late for an important meeting."

"And I'm late for an interview," I chime in, in case it matters.

He pauses to arch a thick eyebrow at me. "An interview? For what position?"

I stand straighter. "I'm sure the likes of you don't

realize this, but the plants in this building don't take care of themselves."

Wait. Have I said too much? Could he torpedo my interview—assuming this elevator snafu hasn't done it already? What does he do here, anyway—design ridiculous elevators? That can't be a full-time job, can it?

"A tree hugger," he mutters under his breath. "That tracks."

What an asshole. I've never hugged a tree in my life. I'm too busy talking to them.

He returns his scowling attention to the "help" button—though now I'm thinking it should've been labeled as "no help."

"Hello? Can you hear me?" he shouts. "Answer now, or you're fired."

I roll my eyes. "Is it a good idea to be a dick to the person who can save us?"

He blows out an audible breath. "It doesn't matter. The button must be malfunctioning. They wouldn't dare ignore me."

I pull out my trusty phone, a nice and simple Nokia 3310. "Full of yourself much?"

He stares at my hands incredulously. "So that's why the elevator got stuck. It went through a time warp and transported us to 2008."

I frown at the lack of reception on my Nokia. "This version was released in 2017."

"It still looks dumber than a brain-dead crash test

dummy." He proudly pulls an iPhone from his pocket. "*This* is what a phone should look like."

I scoff. "That's what constant distraction looks like. Anyway, if your iNotSoSmartPhone—trademarked—is so great, it should have some reception, right?"

He glances at his screen, but I can tell he already knows the truth: no reception for his darling either.

Still, I can't resist. "See? Your genius of a phone is just as useless. All it's good for is turning people into social-media-checking zombies."

He hides the device, like a protective parent. "On top of all your endearing qualities, you're a techno-phobe too?"

I debate throwing my Nokia at his head but decide it's not worth shelling out sixty-five bucks for a replace-ment. "Just because I don't want to be distracted doesn't mean I'm a technophobe."

"Actually, my phone is great at blocking out distractions." He puts the headphones back over his ears. "See?" He presses play, and I hear the faint riffs of heavy metal.

"Very mature," I mouth at him.

"Sorry," he says overly loudly. "I can't hear any distractions."

Fine. Whatever. At least he has good taste in music. My cactus and I are big fans of Metallica, which is what I think he's listening to.

I begin to pace back and forth.

I'm stuck, and I'm late. If this elevator jam doesn't

resolve itself in the next minute or two, I can pretty much kiss the new job goodbye—and by extension, my tuition money. No tuition money means no botany degree, which has been my dream for the last few years.

By saguaro's juices, this sucks really bad.

I sneak a glance at the hottie—I mean, asshole.

What would he say about someone with dyslexia wanting a college degree? Probably that I'd need a university that uses coloring books. In truth, even coloring books wouldn't help that much—I can never stay inside those stupid lines.

I sigh and look away, increasingly worried. My dreams aside, what if the elevator stays stuck for a while?

The most immediate problem is my growing need to pee—but paradoxically, a longer-term worry will be finding liquids to drink.

I wonder... If you're thirsty enough, does your body reabsorb the water from the bladder? Also, could I MacGyver a filter to reclaim the water in my urine with what I have on me? Maybe through cat hair?

I shiver, and only partially from the insane AC that's somehow reaching me even in here. In the short term, it would be so much better if it were hot instead of cold. I'd sweat out the liquids and not need to pee, though I guess I'd die of thirst sooner. I sneak an envious glance at the large stranger. I bet he has a bladder the size of a blimp. He also has a stainless-steel bottle that's probably filled with water that he likely won't share.

There's also the question of food. I don't have anything edible with me, apart from a can of cat food... and, theoretically, the cat herself.

No. I'd sooner eat this stranger than poor Atonic.

As if psychic, the stranger's stomach growls.

Crap. With this guy being so big and mean, he'd probably eat the cat. After that, he'd eat me... and not in a fun way.

I'm so, so screwed.

Chapter 5

Lucius

Why is she prancing around like that? Is she trying to be annoying? Probably, and it's working—to the point where my eyes are feeling itchy from watching her zoom back and forth in this tiny space.

Closing my eyes, I focus on the guitar riffs in my headphones, but somehow, I still feel her presence.

Probably because of how her scent moves around.

She smells like freshly cut grass and sunshine.

I peek through my eyelashes just as she pulls out a CD player from her purse and attaches it to wired headphones.

A CD player? Should I tell her it predates even the antique she calls a phone?

No. Better not to engage. She might sniff out the dissonance of me being so into tech *and* Ancient Rome, and remark that instead of an iPhone, my favorite calculating device should be an abacus.

I sneak another peek. She stops pacing and carefully sets down her huge purse in the corner. The thing looks heavy. I wonder what she keeps in there. A small horror-movie clown/demon, *It* style? A Chucky-esque killer doll?

I rub my increasingly itchy eyes. Another possibility is that she uses the purse as a makeshift sleeping bag. I'm pretty sure she's small enough to fit inside it.

As she resumes her pacing, she fiddles with the controls of the CD player.

I pause my own music to hear what she's listening to.

Hmm. It's just some woman's voice talking.

An audiobook? Do they still make those on CDs?

The one positive thing I can say about my partner-in-jam is that she's done a good job of keeping my mind away from the clusterfuck that is my real estate meeting.

Until now, that is.

Fuck. If I don't get that land, Novus Rome will have another setback, the first one being when those tree huggers raised a stink about deforestation at the original location I chose.

I sigh. Maybe I should've explained to those people how much oxygen would be produced by the vertical greenery I'm planning to cover all the skyscrapers with. Or that I would've planted new trees in Smart Central Park once the construction was over. Or that Novus Rome will strive to have a negative carbon footprint, with self-driving electric cars used as public transport and solar panels covering every surface.

Unfortunately, explaining isn't my strong suit. I can be a tiny bit anti-social, which hurts me in business sometimes. On the plus side, if a zombie apocalypse happened and I had to sit in a bunker by myself, I'd be as happy as a clam on Prozac.

She stops her pacing, visibly shivers, and begins to dance from foot to foot while rubbing her upper arms.

Is she cold?

Probably. She's not wearing all that much, and her creamy skin *is* covered in gooseflesh. Also, her nipples are—

Wait. What am I looking at? Fucking biology strikes again. I have to ignore the—

The lights flicker, then dim further.

Ripping the headphones from my ears, I step over to the help button and stab it again. "Hello? This is Lucius Warren. Do you understand what that means?"

No reply—unless my companion's sneer counts as one.

Grunting in frustration, I look down at her face and can't help but notice how blue her lips are turning.

She's definitely freezing.

"Here." I take off my suit jacket. "Put this on."

She stops her dancing and looks so shocked you'd think I pulled my liver out through my belly button and held it out to her, all bloody and disgusting.

"Your teeth chattering is very annoying," I say coolly. "Do me a favor and put this on."

The fact that it will cover those hard nipples is a bonus.

She doesn't reach for the jacket, just blinks her pretty eyelashes at me.

Speaking of blinking, I do it too, as my eyes feel even itchier.

She still doesn't take the fucking jacket, just stares at me like we're in some cowboy movie standoff. Annoyed, I step around her and wrap her in it.

A huge mistake.

My fingers touch her silky-smooth bare shoulders, and a firehose of endorphins shoots into my bloodstream and circles around all of my appendages before settling right in my dick.

Damn it. On top of everything else, I'm now hard.

Chapter 6

Juno

Holy saguaro.

His strong fingers only touched my skin for a fraction of a second, yet I'm on the verge of turning into a pathetic puddle of need. I blame the scent of the jacket enveloping me—clean, with a hint of almonds, plus something ineffably male.

Needless to say, I feel instantly warm, and not just because the jacket covers me to my knees. Some of this warmth is a side effect of the heat furnace that's come to life between my legs for some reason.

He steps away from me, and my shoulders miss his touch already.

Wait. What the hell am I thinking? The cold must've really scrambled my brains.

Speaking of brain scramble—the way his white shirt clings to his powerful chest doesn't help matters.

Sliding my arms into the jacket sleeves—because I

might as well—I clear my throat. "Thank you, Lucius." As soon as I overheard his name, I couldn't believe I didn't guess it.

He totally looks like a Lucius.

He narrows his eyes at me. "And what's your name?"

"Juno," I say, and brace myself for the usual movie connection.

For the first time since we met—and maybe in his life—his lips quirk in a smile, revealing a dimple. "Ah. Like Juno Sospita."

Wow. I want to live in that dimple. I blink up at him, dazzled, and blurt, "Who?"

The smile is gone without a trace, making me think that I imagined it. In its place is a condescending frown. "Juno the Savior? Queen of the Gods, daughter of Saturn, wife of Jupiter, mother of Vulcan, Mars—"

"Oh, you mean the Roman goddess," I interject, feeling dumb. "Yeah, I know all about her. That's who my parents named me after—her and the month of June, which is when I was born."

Ugh, why am I babbling? He doesn't care when I was born. He probably wishes I'd never been born, judging by the glower on his face.

"For someone named after her, you don't know much," he says. "Like the fact that the month was named after the goddess, so you weren't named after Juno *and* June, just Juno."

26

My hands ball into fists inside the sleeves of his enormous jacket. "I knew that."

"Sure," he says with an eyeroll. "Let's pretend that you did."

"I have a better idea." I put on my headphones. "I'm going to pretend you're not here."

With that, I resume my audiobook and my pacing. I also pretend not to notice him standing there—a difficult task.

He rubs his eyes like they're bothering him, then puts on his headphones as well.

The call of my bladder is getting harder to ignore, but ignore it I must. Because what's the alternative? Ask him to turn away and lift my leg in a corner, like a dog?

He sneezes, startling me.

We lock eyes for a second. Hmm. His steel-gray orbs are red and watery. Is he about to cry over the meeting he's missing?

He pointedly ups the volume on his phone.

Fine.

I up my volume as well, and the indignation helps me pace a while longer. That is, until my bladder is on the verge of bursting like a balloon in the presence of a five-year-old boy with an ice pick. No. Make that like real estate prices circa 2006.

A few minutes later, I'm positive my body *doesn't* know how to utilize the water in my bladder. I'm so thirsty I'm fantasizing about snatching Lucius's water bottle and making a run for it. Which wouldn't work at all inside this tiny elevator.

As if to taunt me, he opens said bottle and takes a big swig.

Ugh. I have to cross my legs to stop myself from peeing with envy.

He takes his headphones off with visible irritation. "Why are you looking at my bottle like that?"

I angrily pause my audiobook. "Like what?"

He gestures at my purse. "Don't you have your own water in that giant bag?"

"No," I say defensively. The thing is heavy thanks to the cat, so I figured I'd get a drink after the interview. I didn't know I'd be stuck here.

He glowers harder, then holds out the water bottle.

I hop from foot to foot and shake my head.

"It's fine," he says, a bit more cordially. "Have a drink."

"I'm okay," I lie.

"Look, if they haven't gotten us already, that means something very serious happened to the elevator, so we might be here a while." He thrusts the bottle my way.

I back away, dancing from foot to foot as I go. "I don't think I should."

He fingers the collar of his shirt. "Are you afraid of my cooties?"

Afraid, no. More like I want to fertilize and water his cooties, until they get big and strong, and then I'd lick them.

"No." My voice breaks, and I clear my parched throat. "Thank you."

He raises one bushy eyebrow. "Why the hell not?"

I clench my thighs together. "None of your business."

He narrows his eyes. "Wait a second." It looks like a giant lightbulb's just exploded into a supernova above his head. "Does it have anything to do with all that dancing around?" He lowers his voice. "Do you need to go?"

My ears, neck, and face feel like someone's rubbed them with pepper spray. "I'm not discussing my bladder with *you*."

He frowns and looks around.

What's he looking for? Is he expecting a ladies' room to magically manifest in the middle of the elevator?

He returns his attention to me, his expression dark. "Okay. So we kill off this bottle, and then you can use it to relieve yourself."

No. No fucking way. Not in front of him.

To which my bladder replies, *Please? For the love of saguaro?*

Ugh. No.

I turn away and try to think of something, anything else. Sand. Death Valley. Saltines. Wait, this is making me even more thirsty.

Damn it.

"It'll be worse if you go in your pants," Lucius says dryly.

Yes, so much worse, my bladder screams. *And it's on the verge of happening!*

No, it's not. I can hold it. I'm not five.

"Alternatively, you could go in your bag," Lucius says helpfully. "Might be easier with your plumbing."

I round on him. "Excuse me? My plumbing?"

He blinks. "What else would you call it?"

Arrgh! Would a jury convict me if I murdered this man? After first waterboarding him with my pee?

"Do not talk about my plumbing," I say through gritted teeth. "Ever."

If only because it's making me think of toilets, thus worsening my bladder's desperate situation.

"Fine." He swishes the water inside the bottle. "If you don't want this, I'm going to finish it myself."

Ouch. Was that a bladder spasm?

I watch through slitted eyes as Lucius tauntingly takes a sip. And another.

"Okay, you win." I stomp over to him and snatch the water bottle from his grasp. My fingers brush his hand in the process, and I almost pee my pants from the zing that travels down my arm. Ignoring it, I clarify, "I mean I'll have some water, not the other thing."

"Sure." He smirks. "Go ahead and finish the rest of it."

I take a greedy swig, and for some reason, he watches my lips intently.

I swallow, and wow. What a relief.

I must've been thirstier than I thought.

When I thrust the empty bottle back at him, he raises his hands. "You keep that. You'll need it."

I roll my eyes and place the bottle on the floor next to my bag.

Okay, no more bending. I almost lost the fight against my bladder just then. The pressure of the water hitting my stomach is worsening my already-dire situation.

A few more minutes and I'm toast. Maybe even seconds.

Lucius arches his eyebrows and looks at me, then at the bottle.

"Stop," I hiss at him. "It's not happening."

"Something is happening. One way or another, nature will win—and you'll either do the unspeakable or have an accident."

I cross my legs and squeeze them, hard. "No way." What sucks is how possible that accident is beginning to sound.

"Just so you know," he says. "Overstretching your bladder can lead to bladder weakness. Not to mention, it's bad for your kidneys. Oh, and I think it can cause cystitis or a UTI, as well as—"

"Do you have a kink or something? You're not getting a golden shower no matter how many urological facts you list."

He flashes his white teeth in a startling grin. "Then

I guess you'd better pray to Cloacina, the Roman toilet goddess." With that pearl of wisdom, he puts on his headphones and turns away.

Fuck. Now that the distraction of the annoying conversation is gone, the urge becomes my whole world. My whole universe.

I don't think I can take it much longer.

Desperate, I put on my audiobook as a last resort and then practice Lamaze breathing with crossed legs.

I also pray in case it helps.

It doesn't.

This is it.

The turning point.

It's either the bottle or my pants.

I eye the bottle.

Can I sneak-pee into it right now?

No. What if he turns?

I clear my throat.

He doesn't hear me.

That's actually good for what's to come, but annoying for now.

I poke him in the shoulder.

He turns and removes one earcup. "What?"

I suck in a breath. "You win."

"I 'win?'" He gestures at the soon-to-be toilet. "That's my favorite water bottle, and I do not have a golden shower kink. If anything—"

"Okay, fine," I grit out. "I lose. You lose. We both lose. Is that better?"

He shrugs.

"I have rules," I say.

Those thick eyebrows of his go up.

"First, I need you to turn away. Then crank up your music as loud as it goes."

His jaw muscle twitches. "You realize that's exactly what I was doing before you interrupted me?"

I clench and unclench my fists, but he can't see it thanks to the giant sleeves of his jacket. "I was afraid you'd turn back before I was done."

He sighs, pointedly turns away, and puts the headphones back on. "There. Tap my shoulder when it's safe to turn."

I roll up my/his jacket's sleeves all the way up to my elbows and make sure the wall he's facing isn't reflective.

It isn't.

I reach into the pocket of my bag and pull out a tiny bottle of hand sanitizer for afterward, being careful not to disturb the cat.

As I drag my feet over to the bottle, I feel like I'm walking the plank.

Is this really about to happen?

If the elevator floor were to collapse or the cables to snap right now, I wouldn't mind all that much.

I unscrew the bottle's lid. Thankfully, it's one of those with a wide mouth, not a sports bottle with a tiny opening.

Seriously, am I doing this?

Seems so.

I turn my back to Lucius, squat, pull down my panties, and position the bottle the best I can.

Wait. When was the last time I ate asparagus?

Nope.

Too late.

The dam breaks, and you could probably power this elevator for a year with the hydroelectric energy produced by the resulting stream.

I will never live this down.

Chapter 7

Lucius

I wait and wait.

And sneeze.

And wait, rubbing my super-itchy eyes.

What's taking so long? Then again, why do I care?

Still, I'd be done twice over by now. Do women take longer than men when it comes to relieving themselves? Is that why they head to the bathroom in groups, so they can kill all that dead time with pleasant conversation?

I suppress the irritation. Given the headache squeezing my temples and the gnawing feeling in my stomach, it's clear that hunger is messing with my head. I may also be coming down with a cold because I have a distinct tickle in my throat and my nose is trying to run. Also, my eyeballs feel like they need to be rubbed with sandpaper, and the urge to sneeze is building again. It's almost as if—

A tiny finger pokes me between my shoulder blades.

Finally.

I face her, keeping my expression neutral. Something tells me that if I smile, she'll turn murderous.

"Did you sanitize that finger before you touched me?" I ask.

She nods.

"Here." Without meeting my gaze, she hands me the capped bottle.

I take a step back. "No, thanks. That's yours to keep."

Without saying a word, she walks over to the giant bag and sets the bottle down on the floor.

My urge to sneeze intensifies. I fight it for as long as I can, but then it happens. I turn away and sneeze. And sneeze again. What the fuck? I locate a tissue in my pocket and manage to catch a third sneeze as she cheerfully says, "Saguaro bless you!" from behind me.

Saguaro, like the cactus?

The idea distracts me enough that I barely catch the fourth sneeze in the tissue. My eyes are full-on running now, and my throat is starting to feel tight. Seriously, what the fuck?

"Are you okay?" she asks, now sounding concerned. "Are you sick?"

Before I can answer, my stomach growls. Loudly.

"Oh, you're hungry," she says.

I turn to glare at her. "Is that your doctorly opinion?" My eyes and nose are killing me.

"I'd be nicer to me if I were you," she says. "I've got food."

My stomach growls louder. "You do?"

"Well." She darts a glance at the bag. "It's really for a more desperate situation. Like if we're here hours from now."

"Oh?"

She exhales. "It's cat food."

My jaw slackens. Did she say *cat* food?

"Hey, I'm not saying I *want* to eat cat food," she says. "But if we have to, this is an organic brand and the main ingredient is chicken. How bad can it be?"

Cat. *That's* what's going on with me.

I point an accusing finger at Juno. "Get away from me. As far as possible."

Her nostrils flare. "What?"

I back up until I'm all the way in the corner. "I'm severely allergic to cats. You must own one, and have its hair or dander on you."

Her eyes widen, and she backs away also. Not that it will help much; we're still less than eight feet apart.

She throws another glance at her bag. "Do you have an EpiPen with you?"

I shake my head. "I don't know if—"

I stop speaking because her bag produces a blood-chilling sound.

A full-blown, actual *meow*.

Chapter 8

Juno

ATONIC'S HEAD POPS OUT.

Okay, so the cat is out of the bag. Literally.

And Lucius is severely allergic.

He's staring at the cat like he can't believe his eyes. "Is that a...?"

"A cat, yes. Afraid so," I say apologetically.

Lucius transfers his incredulous glare to me. "Is this some sort of an assassination attempt?"

My hackles rise again—a default setting when dealing with Lucius. "What are you, a king? A dictator? Kenny from *South Park*?"

Having said that, his death-by-cat would look very natural, as far as assassinations go. The perfect crime. What if this *is* an assassination attempt—just not my doing? Maybe Pearl is not a cheesemaker as she claims, but secretly the top assassin in the world, and she arranged this whole thing: her alleged vacation, her trained killer cat who pretends to sleep until the right moment, this elevator jam—

"Meow?"

Saguaro help us. Atonic leaps out of the bag, and I can picture the whole murder scenario unfolding. She rubs herself on Lucius. He swells up like a teen's peen after a porn video, then clutches at his throat theatrically and goes into anaphylactic shock.

Not on my fucking watch.

"Stay back!" I shout at both of them, and then I bravely put myself between man and beast.

Atonic curls her tail and wags it. Then her ears point forward threateningly, right at Lucius.

"Stay away from him," I say to her sternly.

It's a mistake. Atonic always wants to go exactly where I don't want her to go—most likely a side effect of being a cat. She'll meow next to the bathroom door until I open it, then not go in at all. Though sometimes, she'll just lie on the threshold as if to say, "Bitch, make sure the door remains open at all times." So, in this case, it's clear as day that she really, really wants to rub her allergens directly on her soon-to-be murder victim.

Yep.

She leaps forward.

Luckily for Lucius, there's a reason I was always chosen as the goalie for my high school soccer team.

I snatch the cat mid-leap as Lucius goes into a sneezing fit.

Or at least I try to. A ball of fur behaves quite

differently than a soccer ball, as it turns out. The cat twists free of my grip and lands on her paws—something that balls never do... soccer ones anyway.

Before I can grab her, she goes for him again—but meets my palm, just like that ball did when my team played our biggest rival, Daughters of Chuck Norris.

"It's like it's trying to get me," Lucius says inbetween sneezes. He sounds awful, all congested and annoyed.

"You bring that out in people," I say as I grab for the cat without success. Despite the elevator being a small, enclosed space, I'm having an impossibly hard time catching her.

He scoffs. "Great. Blame the victim."

"Shut up. You're just making her want to get you that much more." Not to mention tempting me to let the cat pass.

The cat gives me a look that seems to say, "Challenge accepted." She tries to snake between my legs—which I close, like a proper lady, before snatching at her without any success.

She tries to get around me on my left. Then on the right. From here, she really picks up steam and tests all of my defensive capabilities, all the while eluding my attempts to catch her and making me wonder if Lucius is made out of catnip.

Given the way he looks, it's possible.

The worst part is that this battle with the cat is making me thirsty again. And tired. I'm not sure how much longer I can defend Lucius at this rate. As a goalie, you're not attacked repeatedly over and over like this—not unless your team is complete shit. Not to mention, it's been thirteen years since I caught any balls... soccer ones, anyway.

Suddenly, the elevator lights go back to their original intensity.

Oh, my. Can it be?

Yes! We begin moving. Heading down instead of up, but that is fine with me.

"Finally," Lucius says triumphantly from behind me before sneezing three times in a row. In a nasally voice, he adds, "Maybe I'll actually survive today."

The extra bonus of the sudden movement is that it seems to confuse the cat, at least for a second, but that is all I need to make my move.

Channeling David Beckham, Michael Jordan, and Mr. Miyagi, I snatch the cat.

I ignore her indignant meows as I grab my purse, stick the cat inside, and close the zipper all the way before slinging the bag over my shoulder.

There. Allergens somewhat contained.

Lucius sneezes again, twice. "Can the cat breathe like that?"

Now he's accusing me of animal cruelty? I turn to say something biting, but at the sight of his red and watery eyes, I settle for, "There are air holes on the sides of the bag. What kind of a monster do you think I am?"

He curses under a sneeze. "Maybe the kind that sneaks a cat into the private elevator of someone who's allergic to them?"

I guess I walked right into that one. But hold on. Did he say a *private* elevator? Who has a private—

The doors open into the lobby, where a crew of firefighters is waiting for us, axes in tow.

"Are you okay?" the tallest one asks as we hurry out of the metal trap. I grab the water bottle on my way and throw it in the nearest trashcan—to hide the evidence.

"What happened?" Lucius demands when he catches his breath after another series of sneezes. "Why was the elevator jammed?"

As the firefighter explains something about a fire in the basement and how it messed up the elevator wiring, I check my phone.

Yep.

I have a pissed-off email from the person I was supposed to meet for the interview. She italicized the part of the email where she stated, "*Needless to say, you aren't getting this job.*"

Is everyone who works in this building so rude? What if I'd been hit by a car?

"Is everyone okay?" Lucius asks the firefighter, surprising me. He sounds a bit better, though still rather congested.

"Yeah," the firefighter says. "A few people inhaled

some smoke, but we got them into the fresh air and they seem to be fine."

"Speaking of fresh air," I chime in. "Lucius, you should get some."

"No. I have an important meeting." He takes out his iPhone and curses at whatever he sees there. "I guess I might as well get that fresh air."

Sounds like his important meeting is as much of a bust as my interview.

He pushes through the firefighters, and I follow, all the way to the front doors.

To my surprise, Lucius holds them open for me. Probably to speed up the process of getting me—and the cat—out of his life.

I still thank him as I pass and make sure not to touch him with the bag containing the cat.

He doesn't acknowledge my gratitude, probably because he's too busy glowering at a couple of people with cameras.

Hey, it's interesting not to be the target of his ire for a change.

I check out the strangers. They look like reporters, or maybe paparazzi. Either way, how bad was that basement fire to draw them here? I didn't think either group even covered fires.

"Mr. Warren," says a man who looks the most like a weasel—and his competition is stiff. "Is that—"

"No comment," Lucius says sharply.

The guy doesn't look the least bit surprised by the rebuke. Lifting his camera, he joins his brethren in taking pictures of Lucius—and, thanks to proximity, of me.

I blink at the bright flashes and frown.

Who is Lucius that paparazzi-types want to take his picture?

Ignoring the cameras, Lucius waves at a limo parked nearby.

An older man with the stiff upper lip of a butler exits the vehicle and opens the back door.

"This is Elijah," Lucius says to me. Turning to Elijah, he commands, "Take Juno home."

I'm getting a ride in a limo? Seriously?

Who *is* this man?

"What about you, sir?" Elijah asks, predictably with a British accent.

Lucius replies with a glare.

"Consider it done, sir," Elijah says with a courtly bow.

"Lucius must be a pure joy to work for," I say to Elijah in a conspiratorial tone as I approach the vehicle. I'm not about to turn down a free ride after everything I've just been through.

The corners of Elijah's eyes smile, but the rest of his face looks dignified, stern in its butler-ness. "Have a seat, please."

"Hold on." I carefully place my bag on the floor of the limo. "I have to give Lucius his jacket back.

Lucius wrinkles his nose. "Don't."

Is he nuts? It must be expensive, and I'll have no use for it.

"Seriously, take it back." I slide my arms out of the sleeves. "If it's about the cat cooties, I'll pay for dry cleaning."

Lucius turns to Elijah. "Dispose of that."

Elijah takes the jacket and gestures for me to get inside the limo.

I do so, and only after he closes the door do I fully process just how weird this is.

Why is Lucius giving me a limo ride in the first place? Isn't he worried he'll have to fumigate the car afterward on account of my cat companion?

Elijah gets behind the wheel. "Madam, what's the address?"

Madam? Does he think I own a brothel?

I tell him where to go and think of questions to ask about Lucius, but before I can fire away, the partition between us goes up and the car departs.

Fine.

Whatever.

Mentally preparing to get my eyes clawed out, I open the bag.

Of course. Atonic is catatonic once again. It's like she knows the allergic asshole is outside her claws' grasp.

I check on my messages and find one from Pearl informing me that she wants to reunite with her fur baby tomorrow, on her way home from the airport.

Yeah, sure, I text back. *Remind me to tell you about the murder she almost committed.*

Pearl replies right away:

I'm going to lose reception in a second, or else I'd make you tell me NOW.

I grin. Pearl lives for three things: this cat, making cheese, and gossip.

———

The moment the limo stops, Elijah opens the door for me.

"How did you get here from your seat so fast?" I ask.

His eyebrows, nearly as thick as Lucius's, lift. "Fast?"

"Are you secretly the Flash?"

"If we're talking DC Universe, don't you think I'm more of an Alfred?" he asks, deadpan.

I conceal a smile. "If your secret isn't speed, is it possible there are two of you—identical twins working to create this effect?"

"I'm just good at my job," maybe-Elijah says. "And you have a fanciful imagination."

I climb out of the car. "Well, sure. Keep your secrets, and thanks for the ride. Oh, and please tell Lucius it was a pleasure meeting him... not."

This time, Elijah's smile actually touches his lips.

"Mr. Warren isn't as bad as the first impression makes one think."

"This one agrees to disagree." I grab my bag and head in the direction of my building. "Thanks again, and toodles."

———

"So," I croon to El Duderino when I've settled in my place. "I must tell you about my crazy day." I proceed to share everything because who needs a therapist when there's a cactus around?

Dude, that's totally radical. This Lucius dude sounds like a dude you should stay away from.

El Duderino is my beavertail cactus who, in my opinion, doesn't look like a beaver (either the animal or the sex organ) or its tail. His kind are native to the Mojave, Anza-Borrego, and Colorado deserts—and don't ask me why he sounds like a water-loving surfer in my mind.

"I couldn't agree more," I reply to him out loud. "I will definitely stay away from Lucius."

Of course you'd agree, dude. It's like your voice is my voice... dude.

I'll admit, I might be a little too into cactuses. But hey, at least if someone tries to rob my place, they'll end up looking like a pincushion.

I check El Duderino's soil. Yep. It's been three

weeks since I watered him last, and today is the big day.

I pour lukewarm water into a saucer and place it underneath El Duderino's pot.

Wow, dude. That's a big wave. Radical.

"I'm glad you like it."

Dude! At this rate, I'll totally flower in a week or so.

As the water absorbs into El Duderino's soil, I feed the cat and check for new job prospects. There are none. Today was my big opportunity, and I blew it. Or the elevator did.

Dude, I'm totes cool on the agua.

I check. Yep. Soil is just right. I remove the saucer.

Thanks, dude. Drowning is a totally uncool way to go.

"Okay. My time for nourishment," I say and start on my own dinner.

Afterward, I watch some TV, pet Atonic, talk to El Duderino one last time, and head to bed. As I fall asleep, I make it a point not to think of—or dream about—a certain man I was stuck in an elevator with.

No matter how tempting it might be.

———

A doorbell startles me awake.

Grr. Lucius was just licking my—

Wait. Maybe it's good I was awoken from *that*.

As usual, the cat is sleeping on top of my head,

probably pretending to be one of those wigs the nobility wore in yesteryear.

I carefully move her aside and rush to brush my teeth before sprinting for the door.

When I open it, Pearl is standing there, green eyes wide and excited.

"You're famous!" She thrusts her phone at my face.

I rub my eyes. "What are you—"

And then I see it.

A picture of me and Lucius underneath a headline:

Billionaire Recluse Finally Gets a Girlfriend

What the saguaro-fucking fuck?

Chapter 9

Lucius

I SPEND a couple hours dealing with the fallout from the fire before I'm able to grab a conference room with Eidith to talk about the Novus Rome land clusterfuck.

"Smithson left after a half-hour wait," Eidith says without preamble. Then, for some odd reason, she puts her hand on my elbow as she adds, "He said he had another offer, and that he'd take it."

I resist the urge to shake off her hand and smash my palm on the conference room desk. "Why? He has to know I'd offer more."

She pulls her hand away, thankfully, and shrugs. "Your being late hurt his ego. Probably thought you weren't serious."

Fucking real estate moguls and their egos. "You couldn't talk him down?"

As she shakes her head, not a single hair falls out of place on her sprayed-into-submission hairdo.

That's that then. Eidith has excellent people skills, and if she can't influence someone, no one can. She's got the instincts of a shark, and I rely on her often in situations like this.

I decide to cut my losses and move on. There is another possibility I've been mulling over, anyway. "What about that other plot of land? The one in central Florida?"

She wrinkles her nose minutely. "I can set it up, but are you sure? They get hurricanes."

"And we get fires. And earthquakes."

"Great point, as always." She takes out her phone. "I'll get in touch with them."

Okay. Maybe Florida will work even better than California. After all, everyone compares Novus Rome to a theme park—which it most definitely won't be. But if it were, Orlando is just as famous for theme parks as Southern California, if not more so. The climate is also warm, and labor would be cheaper. And if we needed to cut down any trees, there'd likely be less pushback there.

For the rest of the day, I revisit my plans to see what changes I'd have to make if the location were Florida. Turns out, there are very few.

Tired, I go home, eat dinner, and decide to unwind. As always, that involves some facetime with my favorite creatures in the whole world: Caligula, Blackbeard, and Malfoy.

Crossing the pool area, I step into the giant air-conditioned greenhouse they call home.

The trio greets me with happy sounds and sideways hops as soon as I enter.

Feeling the tension melt away, I bend to pet each one. The petting quickly morphs into frantic play. The trio sleeps sixteen hours a day, but when they finally wake up, they have the kind of energy that humans can reach only by using deadly doses of amphetamines.

"Hi, sir," says Vincent, the veterinarian I hired to watch after them while I'm at work. "No health problems to report today."

I look up. "Did Caligula learn to roll over?"

He nods. "I reinforced it in the others too."

I decide to take him at his word. "Caligula, roll over."

He does as he is told. Then Blackbeard and Malfoy join in, and it turns into a rolling game.

"Great job," I say to everyone, including Vincent.

"Is it okay if I go pick out some toys for enrichment?" Vincent asks.

I wave him away and focus on my charges as they start a chase—only they do it sideways, because they're ferrets.

Not for the first time, I wish I could bring them with me to places, the way Juno does with her cat. Alas, that wouldn't go well. At best, they'd steal every small object at my office, and at worst, they'd shred themselves in a paper shredder. Also, as far as the state of California's government is concerned, my trio of ferrets is the "Ferrets of Rome Conservation Society." My lawyers had to form this legal entity because ferrets are illegal to own as pets here. You need a special permit to keep them, which is only given to zoos, universities with veterinary research programs, and conservation societies.

Why did I get ferrets in the first place?

I didn't.

My mother bought them on a whim in Las Vegas, only to decide not to keep them after they hid all the knickknacks in her apartment. Giving up instead of nurturing is as typical a behavior for my mother as stealing is for the ferrets. In fact, the term "ferret" is based on the Latin *furittus*, which translates to *little thief*. Romans kept them instead of cats to hunt mice.

My phone vibrates in my pocket.

I take it out carefully. Blackbeard has stolen it from me at least five times, Caligula four, and Malfoy has not only stolen it a dozen times but has also broken it twice.

"Hi, Gram." I lift the phone to my ear as small paws snatch for it skillfully. Yes, there's a ferret climbing up my body, and I don't mind. "How are you?"

"Why didn't you tell me you had a girlfriend?" Gram sounds disappointed, a rarity in our interactions.

What is she talking about? I grab Blackbeard off my head and put him on the floor next to the other two. They look at me, seemingly as puzzled as I am. As intelligent as they are, they have no idea what Gram is talking about either.

"What do you mean, 'girlfriend?'" I ask carefully.

"A girlfriend is that thing I've been telling you to get," Gram says. "One that leads to fiancée, then to wife, then to great-grandkids."

I shake my head, then realize she can't see me. "I don't have a girlfriend."

All the women I've met in recent years have viewed me as a piggybank with a cock, and in return, I think of them as nothing more than a way to silence biology. It was worse when I was younger and money-less, though. They didn't see me as anything at all.

"Don't be coy," Gram says sternly. "It's all over the internet."

Caligula nibbles on my shoe as I pull my phone away to gape at it.

"Hello?" Gram's tinny voice sounds from the speaker. "You there?"

"I'm going to need to call you back," I say, bringing the phone back to my ear.

"No way, mister. I demand—"

"Two minutes." Before she can object, I end the call—the first time I've hung up on her in my life.

A text from Gram arrives instantly, sparing me from having to Google myself—which is why I got off the phone. The message contains an emoji of two revolving hearts and a link to an article with a picture of me and Juno coming out of my building, along with enough lies to make the most crooked politician proud.

I grit my teeth as I scan the article. The author is that idiot reporter. I've turned down his bungling attempts to interview me, but he hasn't given up and stalks me like I'm some dumb celeb. Does he not realize that I could buy his tawdry publication and fire him with one phone call? Or have my security team dig up all kinds of dirt on him and have it published in the—

My phone vibrates again.

I pick up on autopilot as Malfoy takes his turn nibbling at my foot.

"See, I know everything," Gram says. "And I'm so happy. The happiest I've been in a long time."

I shake my head—which doesn't clear it. "You're happy?"

"Of course," she says with a girlish giggle. "When I heard the news, I got so excited my blood pressure dropped."

I snatch my foot away before Caligula bites it. His teeth are the sharpest of the three, and I happen to like the shoes I have on. "I'm pretty sure that's supposed to go the other way."

"Nope. It dropped. Also, I've been feeling pretty weak lately, but I didn't tell you so you wouldn't worry. But as soon as I read that article, I felt ten years younger."

Here we go again.

"Say you'll introduce the two of us," Gram wheedles. "Can you imagine how much such a meeting would improve my health?"

Yep. She's manipulating me. This is signature Gram. I'm certain this health stuff is total bullshit, but one day, it might not be. She's under the care of the best doctors, but still, she's in her eighties. If I ever ignored one of her requests and her health declined afterward, I'd never forgive myself.

Except I can't give her this one. I can't have her meet my non-existent girlfriend. Unless... A crazy idea flits through my mind.

"Seriously," Gram says. "Please let me meet her. I need to make sure she's good enough for my pumpkin."

I sigh, loudly. "I'll have to think about this."

"What's there to think about?" she asks querulously. "Are you ashamed of your Gram?"

She is really laying it on thick today. "I'm not ashamed." As I say this, I decide that maybe the idea is not so crazy after all. Pivoting with the same swiftness I apply to business, I say evenly, "It's just that this thing is new. I don't want Juno to feel like things are moving too fast."

"Her name is Juno?" Gram sounds as excited as my ferrets are acting. "I love that name!"

"It's a nice name." Unlike the *owner* of the name, but Gram doesn't need to know that.

"Okay," Gram says. "If it's too soon, I'll wait. But keep in mind, I'm not a spring chicken."

This again? She *really* wants this.

"I should go," I say. "Juno is probably expecting my call."

Gram gasps. "Oh, no! Call her. Immediately."

Is that panic in her voice? Seriously? "Okay. I'll call."

"Good. Don't mess this up," Gram warns and hangs up without a goodbye.

Just like in business, I analyze the decision I've reached quickly, all the pros and cons aligning neatly in my head.

Pros: Gram will be happy—and maybe, though unlikely, healthier too. Another benefit, albeit a minor one: this should reduce the number of gold diggers I have to dodge at events. Also, it might make me more relatable to certain types of people, thus smoothing the way for some business transactions.

Cons: I'll have to deal with Juno, and by extension, that nightmare of a cat.

So, it's decided. I will make Juno my girlfriend. A pretend girlfriend, obviously. Now I just need to do some due diligence to make sure she isn't married and doesn't have too many skeletons in her closet. To that end, I get in touch with my Head of Security and explain the situation.

"What do we know about her?" he asks.

"Her first name is Juno," I say. "Elijah dropped her off at her place, so we have her address. Oh, and she was in the building for some plant-care-related job interview."

"That's plenty to go on," he says. "Do you want the usual dossier?"

"Just check for any red flags and make it fast."

He assures me that he's on it and hangs up.

I refocus my attention on the ferrets.

Blackbeard is dragging a garden glove that he stole from who knows where, Caligula's head is buried in the lilac planter, and Malfoy is nipping Caligula's nipple, one cringingly close to his "bellybutton."

I shake my head, watching them. Some people—including my own mother—like to kiss said "bellybutton," or gently poke it, or tickle it, or rub it, or blow raspberries into it. Hopefully, they do it without realizing the biological reality that when it comes to male ferrets, what seems like their "bellybutton" is actually their penis.

Seriously, I can't wait until our brains are integrated with computers. Maybe then, most humans won't be so dumb.

Chapter 10

Juno

"Tell me everything." Pearl's exaggeratingly demanding tone and the way she strokes her cat conspire to make her resemble an evil villain—or to reveal her true nature. "And I mean every detail," she continues. "Or else."

With a sigh, I gesture for her to sit on my raggedy couch and launch into it, pacing around the tiny space of my studio. For self-preservation reasons, I do not mention the water bottle incident or the wet dreams Pearl interrupted by showing up so early.

"So... you didn't know that Lucius Warren is one of the richest men in the country?" She says this with such passion Atonic stops being catatonic and gives me a lazy once-over from her lap. "The closest an American can get to being a prince?"

I shake my head, still stunned by that bizarre article.

"Or that he owns the building you were interviewing in?"

Another headshake. I feel dumb about this one because he did have the attitude of someone who owned that elevator. And the building, and the people, and the sky above it all. In hindsight, it makes sense that he turned out to be a billionaire—a reclusive, grumpy one at that.

Why on earth would anyone think I'm his girlfriend?

Pearl's eyes drill into me. "And you are absolutely, positively sure you guys are not dating?" The disappointment she's channeling rivals that of *Star Wars* fans when they first saw Jar Jar Binks.

I roll my eyes. "The reporter totally made the whole thing up. By now, Lucius has probably forgotten all about me."

My doorbell rings.

Pearl arches an eyebrow. "Expecting anyone?"

I throw a suspicious glance at the door. "No."

She leaps to her feet. "Let's go see who it is."

I check the peephole and gasp.

It can't be.

I rub the eye that just tried to fool me and check again.

By saguaro's spines, it's Elijah—the driver of the billionaire we were just discussing.

I open the door.

Yep. Still Elijah.

"Hi," is what comes out of my mouth.

"Morning," he replies.

If this is a hallucination, it's not just visual anymore.

I dart a glance at Pearl. Given her confused expression, she's seeing the same thing I am.

Okay then, Lucius's butler is here. At my door.

"Introduce us," Pearl whispers loudly enough for the neighbors to hear.

"Sorry," I say. "This is Elijah. He works for Lucius Warren."

Pearl's eyes widen. "Oh. Will you invite him in?"

Oh, right. "Please come in."

Elijah darts a glance at the cat. "I was instructed not to get any cat on myself."

"Oh, the cat was just leaving," Pearl says.

"Indeed?" Elijah looks like she's promised him peace on Earth.

"She's actually *my* pet," Pearl says with a wink. "So your employer doesn't need to worry about allergies when he hangs out with Juno."

Gah. Even after all the reassurances I gave her about us not dating, that is where her mind goes.

"I'm sure this will come as great news to him," Elijah says with a bow to Pearl. Turning to me, he says, "He sent me to say that he is eager to speak with you when you have an opportune moment."

I blink stupidly at everyone. "Eager... to speak with me?"

"Probably about the article," Pearl says helpfully.

Oh. Shit. I didn't even think about that. Am I in some kind of trouble? Is he? Is there a special FBI task force out there that polices the dating life of bad-tempered billionaires?

I bite my lip. "I guess I can talk to him." Nodding at Pearl, I add, "If he kills me, I have a witness now."

"Wonderful." Elijah grabs a giant box off the floor by my door and hands it to me. "Mr. Warren kindly requested you wear this."

In a stupor, I grab the box and look inside—as does my nosy best friend.

I'm not sure if I expected it to contain the cut-off head of the paparazzi who took our picture, the cut-off head of the person responsible for the elevator jam, or a portable potty in case I need to pee in Lucius's presence again, but I definitely did *not* expect a dress, shoes, and undergarments.

"Wow," Pearl says.

"Versace and Gucci," Elijah says. "If I'm not mistaken."

I take the dress out and gape at it, then repeat the action with the shoes and the undies. Each item is more expensive than anything in my place, including possibly the apartment itself. "What's all this for?"

Pearl rips her envious gaze from the dress to look at me. "Seems like someone wants his girlfriend to look nice in the next picture... as well as in the bedroom."

Elijah purses his lips. "Mr. Warren wanted to

provide something new for you to wear out of concern for his allergies."

"Oh," Pearl says, her disappointment palpable. "I probably should take the cat out of here, before I ruin that part of the plan."

Elijah steps out of her way.

"Wait a second," I say, pinching the bridge of my nose. "No one is going anywhere until someone explains to me what Lucius wants."

Despite what Elijah has said, I can't help but think that the underwear implies something inappropriate, though it's possible Pearl has just primed me.

Elijah's expression turns inscrutable. "I cannot say. I'm not privy to Mr. Warren's confidences."

"He wants *you*," Pearl says. "Obviously."

That can't be it. Impossible. But he does want *something,* and if I don't learn what, the curiosity is going to kill me.

I guess I a*m* going with Elijah—especially since I'm dying to try on the dress and the shoes, and the only socially acceptable way to do that is to agree to this craziness.

Wait a second. I examine the items I'm holding. "How did he know my sizes?"

Pearl waggles her eyebrows obscenely. "He 'sized you up,' obviously. A keeper, that one."

"Nothing like that," Elijah says. "He had his security team do a little research into you. That's how I knew which apartment door to ring as well."

A security team figured out my bra size? How? And more importantly, why? Not to mention, the guy has a *security team*?

"So alpha," Pearl breathes in awe. "Total keeper."

Yeah, if by that she means an asshole who casually invades your privacy. Maybe that FBI task force exists for a reason.

"Okay." I put everything back in the box. "I'm going to go try this on, and if I like how I look, maybe I'll speak with him."

Elijah clears his throat, looking very uncomfortable. "Mr. Warren has a request that's a prerequisite to everything else."

I sigh. "What is it? Did his security team forget to tell him what brand of tampons I use?"

Elijah blushes like a maiden. "Could you wash the cat from your skin and hair?"

"Excuse me?" I feel my face pinching like a crab claw. "He wants me to shower?"

Pearl grins. "I bet his exact words to Elijah were, 'Bathe her and bring her to me.'"

Elijah's blush deepens. "Once again, this is about medical safety."

Is it, though? He survived being in an elevator with me 'dirty,' not to mention with the cat menace herself. Still, I *was* planning to shower since I happen to do that every morning, so no point in discomfiting poor Elijah further.

"I'll take the stinking shower," I say grudgingly.

64

"And I'll take the cat out of here," Pearl says. "Before the unthinkable happens and a cat hair lands where it shouldn't."

"Would you mind if I disinfected your apartment in the meantime?" Elijah asks me.

My initial impulse is an angry rebuke, but then I realize I'm about to get a free apartment cleaning. "Why the hell not?" I say with a sigh.

"That reminds me," Pearl says. "Where is Atonic's litterbox?"

I tell her and stomp to the shower.

———

As the limo drives through Malibu, I can't help but reflect on how annoyingly perfect the dress, the shoes, and especially the undies feel.

It's like those designers custom-made them for me.

Grr. What if this ruins TJMaxx clothes for me? Relatedly, what if these limo rides ruin Uber for me? Or—

We stop, and Elijah does that trick where he opens the door for me impossibly quickly.

"Thanks." I step out and take in the glorious view of the ocean. "Is that the place?" I gesture at a beach-front restaurant that's so fancy and expensive that the closest people like me can get to it is reading about it in *The Michelin Guide*. Which I have.

"Indeed," Elijah says. "Mr. Warren is already inside."

Okay. Here goes. I click-clack over there in my new pumps, my blood pressure rising as I picture myself facing off with Lucius again.

"Ms. Lazko," says the hostess. "Please follow me."

Should I even bother getting surprised that she knows who I am?

She leads me through a completely empty restaurant until we reach the table with the best view.

Lucius is waiting there, a glass of wine in his hand. For some bizarre reason, my breath catches, and I feel warm in all the wrong places.

Suppressing my wayward libido, I tear my eyes away from how his suit jacket hugs his broad shoulders and get straight to the point. "You bought me a bra and panties?"

Lucius looks me over from head to toe, his expression unreadable, while the hostess sounds like she's choking on her saliva as she says, "I'll tell the chef to start the omakase."

"Do so," Lucius says to her with a dismissive wave of his hand before standing up to pull out a chair, presumably for me.

I plant my butt in said chair. "Don't dodge my question."

"I'm not." He returns to his seat. "The answer is obviously yes."

By saguaro's roots, he's set a new record for

bringing out my violent urges. "You don't deny being completely inappropriate?"

"Is this how you always react to gifts? You must be a joy on your birthday."

"There are appropriate gifts, and there are inappropriate gifts," I grit out.

He lifts a thick eyebrow. "So... you're not wearing the bra and panties I bought you?"

"None of your business."

His pupils dilate slightly. "Are you wearing *any* underwear?"

"That's even less of your business!"

He cocks his head. "I claim you *are* wearing my gift. Want to deny it?"

Grr. A tingly sensation circumnavigates from the back of my neck all the way across my face. "If I *am* wearing anything, it would be because Elijah played the cat allergy card."

His expression darkens. "That reminds me... Who carries their friend's cat to an interview? Or anywhere?"

When did he hear about Pearl? Was this also part of the info his security team dug up? Elijah doesn't seem like the text-and-drive type.

I massage my suddenly stiff neck. "Don't try to make this about me. Apart from the undies, you also have to answer for the invasion of my privacy."

Before he can reply, our waiter—a tall, handsome

guy about my age—comes over with a bottle of wine and two glasses.

"1996 Screaming Eagle," he says, displaying the bottle like he's in a magazine ad.

Lucius nods, and the waiter uncorks the wine and pours a glass for him.

When it's my turn, the waiter sneaks an appreciative glance over me. I blink, equal parts surprised and flattered, but then I remember what I'm wearing. My newfound attractiveness is due to Versace and Gucci... and Lucius for buying the outfit.

Speaking of Lucius, his eyes are flinty all of a sudden—and zeroed in on the waiter. "Where is the waitress?"

The waiter sets down the wine and looks like he's about to bolt. "Which one do you mean? We have several."

"The blonde," Lucius says imperiously. "The one with good memory."

"Jessica?" the waiter asks cautiously.

"Whatever," Lucius says. "Where is she?"

Should I feel less special now that I see Lucius is a rude bastard not just to me?

The waiter backs away from the table. "When someone books the whole restaurant, I'm the one who—"

"Get someone else." The sentence sounds like a military order.

The waiter glances helplessly at the hostess. "How about Maddy? Everyone else is—"

"That's fine." Lucius reaches into his pocket and takes out a crisp hundred-dollar bill. "For your trouble."

The waiter snatches the money and rushes over to the hostess.

Their conversation is easy to picture:

"Maddy, you pulled the short straw today."

"No, Hot Waiter, I don't want to serve that guy. Please don't make me."

"He tips in hundreds."

"Fine. But I bet I'll feel like I earned every penny by the time their meal is done."

With the conversation over, the hostess-turned-waitress and the handsome waiter head over to the kitchen.

"You realize they'll spit in our food now," I whisper.

Lucius scoffs. "If anyone dares to spit in the masterpiece that the chef has so carefully crafted, he'll carve them into sashimi."

My palms feel twitchy, like they want to smack someone. "You made me look bad by association."

He swirls the wine in his glass. "How?"

I pick up my own glass lest I actually do smack him. "By being an ass?"

He takes a sip. "He was unprofessional, and I didn't fire him. An ass would have."

I put my glass down. "Wait. You own this place?"

He shrugs. "When you taste the black cod, you'll see why."

Unable to come up with a rebuttal that isn't filled with expletives, I pick up my glass and take a sip of the wine.

Holy grapes. I'm not a connoisseur, but this is by far the best wine I've ever tasted. It's feather light, silky smooth, and has an earthy aftertaste I can't quite place.

"You like wine?" Lucius asks, watching me intently.

I didn't think I did, but maybe I do now. "You're still changing the subject."

His expressive eyebrows ask a question.

"My privacy," I enunciate. "You invaded it."

"You realize you applied for a job with a company I own?" he asks.

I squint at him. "So?"

"What my team did isn't all that different from the background check you would've gotten from any employer."

I catch my fingers tapdancing on the tabletop and stop them. "That's done before offering someone a job."

He sets down his glass. "Why do you think you're here?"

I'm so stunned by the question that I gulp my wine, tasting none of its earlier subtleties.

Something like, "Why am I here?" should've been

the first question I asked, but somehow, I find it hard to do the logical thing when Lucius is around.

As I open my mouth to finally ask that important question, the waitress/hostess, Maddy, sashays over to our table with a tray in her hands.

"Lobster tartare," she says as she sets two plates in front of each of us. Batting her fake eyelashes at Lucius, she demurely adds, "Was there a reason you asked for me to serve you, Mr. Warren?"

Jeez, lady, have some dignity.

"I merely wanted a professional," Lucius says coolly. "Someone who doesn't ogle the customer's dates."

Does he not realize the irony of saying that to a woman actively ogling him as they speak? She doesn't know I'm not really his date, despite what he's just said.

Maddy does seem to be quick on the uptake because she halts her own ogling instantly and mumbles something that sounds like, "Understood, sir."

As soon as she leaves, Lucius nods at the lobster. "I want your opinion."

Feeling like I'm in *The Twilight Zone*, I stab some lobster on my plate and dip it into the buttery sauce.

The flavor explosion in my mouth is so surprisingly pleasurable I have to bite my lip to suppress a moan.

Lucius watches me with his signature intensity. "Well?"

"It's good," I say in an understatement of the century.

With a self-satisfied nod, he eats some of his own dish, making the action look so annoyingly sensual that for a second, I wish I were a lobster. When he swallows, he nods again, approvingly.

"Now," I say as my hand spears more lobster onto my fork of its own accord. "Why are we here?"

Chapter 11

Lucius

SHE FORKS the piece of lobster into her mouth, and I curse biology once again for making such a benign action distracting.

"Have you read the gossip about us?" I ask, wrenching my mind away from her delectable lips with effort.

Still chewing, she nods.

"That saves time." I look her in the eyes—a technique Eidith suggested for when I want to show people I'm about to say something very important. "I want us to play along with that gossip."

She swallows the lobster with an audible gulp, and in my mind, I see a whole sequence of events play out: she chokes, I get behind her and do the Heimlich (in the least pervy way possible), she's grateful for her life and—

"What?" she asks, not choking in the slightest.

I shut the door on the bizarre fantasy and refocus on the conversation. "I want the world to think we're dating."

She dabs her mouth with a napkin. "Me and you... dating?" Her face takes on a delicious pink glow. "That's the most ridiculous idea I've ever heard."

I rub my temples. As is now becoming a tradition, talking to her is giving me a headache. "For a change, I agree with you. Us dating is ridiculous, but nevertheless, that is what we will be pretending to do."

She leaps to her feet. "Like hell we will."

Unsure of what the gentlemanly action would be, I stand up too. "I'll pay you a lot more than what you would've made at the job you didn't get."

She backs away from the table. "You want to pay me to date you?"

I open my mouth to tell her how stupid that question is, but then I close it to avoid further escalation. The last thing I want is for her to run out of the restaurant. "Not date me. *Pretend* to date me. The difference is huge."

Her nostrils flare. "The difference is one between a prostitute and an escort."

"It's more like acting," I say. "There won't be any physical component to our pretense."

The waitress—what was her name?—comes out of the kitchen and doesn't blink an eye as she places small plates of the chef's signature black cod on the table before sprinting away.

"Will you sit?" I say, doing my best to keep my voice even. "This dish is worth it."

"No." She punctuates her point by stomping her distractingly perfect foot, like a fucking toddler.

I can feel my headache pulsing through a vein in my forehead. "We both know you need tuition money."

Great. She looks like she might turn into a fire-breathing dragon. "How do you know that?"

"The alleged invasion of your privacy that you berated me about. Did you already forget?"

She lifts her chin. "I'll make the money another way."

"Oh?" I told myself I wasn't going to play dirty, but that's out the window now. "Do you think you'll get a job now?"

She pales. "What do you mean? I *will* get a job, if not with your company, then elsewhere."

I shrug. "What if word gets out about how inappropriately you behave in public places... such as elevators?"

She staggers back, green eyes wide. "You wouldn't." She presses a tiny fist to her mouth. "What am I saying? Of course you would."

I obviously wouldn't, but she doesn't need to know that.

"Will you sit so we can discuss this like civilized people?"

Looking defeated, she plants her backside on her chair, and I mirror her action.

"How much money are we talking about?" she asks warily.

I add a zero to the number I originally had in mind and tell her.

Her eyes widen again. She knows that's enough to cover four years at any university—including tuition and all other expenses, with quite a bit left over.

To my surprise, she recovers quickly. "Double that, and I'll think about it."

"Done." If only to reward her impressive negotiating skills. Her poker face is better than most I've seen in the boardroom.

"Elaborate on the lack of a physical component," she says, and the poker face cracks a tiny bit—probably because she finds the idea of doing anything with me disgusting.

Trying not to dwell on that, I ask, "What would be the bare minimum required to sell this illusion?"

Her forehead creases. "That would depend on how much time we spend in public."

"I'd say expect the maximum time we can spend together without murdering one another."

"Ten minutes," she says with a snort, then stabs her fork into her cod and sticks it in her mouth.

I follow her example.

Delicious. This dish alone makes this restaurant worth the extravagant price I paid for it.

Realizing I've closed my eyes in pleasure, I open them to see a blissed-out expression on Juno's face too.

Is that what she looks like post-orgasm?

Fucking biology. Why should I care about her O-face, sexy though it might be?

She swallows reverently. "I'm tempted to change our deal. On top of the money, I want this dish for every single meal until I get sick of it, assuming that's even possible."

I chuckle despite myself. "It's been five years for me, and I'm not sick of it yet."

Smiling, she finishes her piece, and I make the mistake of watching her.

Fuck. I like both her smile and that second O-face —or whatever you call it.

I know she was joking about that adjustment to our deal, but I'd throw that in—provided I could watch her eat.

No. She's skittish even with a purely platonic arrangement. Something like "I want to watch you eat" would be as odd as me demanding that "I shall massage your feet anytime I want"—another stipulation that may have crossed my mind.

She downs what remains of her wine. "Okay. With minimal public appearances and PDA, I think I could be your stupid girlfriend... for three times the number you named earlier."

"You have yourself a deal." I take out a folded bundle of papers from my suit jacket's inner pocket. "This is the contract and the NDA. Have your lawyer review it and get back to me."

"Right, *my lawyer*." She snatches the papers so fast she nearly gives us both papercuts. "Her Honorable Imaginariness will jump right on it."

"You want a down payment so you can hire someone?"

She blinks, then nods. "That would be great. Also... I just thought of a new condition."

The waitress comes back with the geoduck clam dish, and I wait for her to leave before I ask, "What's the condition?"

Juno eyes the new dish skeptically, then locks eyes with me. "You can never—*ever*—mention what happened in that elevator again. That's my version of an NDA."

I resist the urge to grin. "If that's your wish."

She narrows her eyes. "I mean it. The deal is off if you so much as mention elevators. Or bottles."

The fight against the grin is impossibly difficult now. "What about cats?"

She rolls her eyes. "You can talk about cats."

"How about Roman numerals?"

"No," she says sternly. "Roman numerals are where I draw the line."

Chapter 12

Juno

Do I see a hint of that dimple? That should probably also go on the no-no list—especially if keeping things platonic is important to him.

To take my mind off the urge to lick said dimple, I shake the paperwork. "Can you explain this in plain English? Translate from the legalese for me."

He does so as we devour the penis-like clam dish and the next course—a ridiculously delicious plate of wagyu beef. Basically, I just have to keep my mouth shut about our arrangement to everyone, even my family. Which, for the money he's paying, I'm happy to do.

"That all sounds as reasonable as such things could," I say when he's done talking. I spear the last bit of the beef, already mourning its absence. "Now, tell me why."

He pours us both more wine. "Why what?"

I shrug, unsure of where to start. "Why me? Why not get a real girlfriend? Why would you fake a relationship? Why—"

The waitress returns, so I stop my torrent of questions.

"Crab meatball soup," she announces and scurries away.

Lucius grabs a spoon. "You must try this."

The soup smells divine, but I don't let that distract me. "You *really* like to change the subject."

His Adam's apple bobs—temptingly, I might add. "What subject am I changing?"

"Why me?" I repeat, then grab my spoon and fill my mouth with some broth and meatball. Maybe if I'm quiet, he'll feel the need to fill the silence.

Nope. He just joins me in eating. Ass.

I judged too soon, though. After swallowing, he surprises me by saying, "The 'why you?' is very simple. You are the person the gossip articles shipped me with."

Oh, yeah. He even started this whole thing by asking if I've read the gossip about us. I feel so special now. My girlfriend qualifications seem to be: has a head and was at the wrong place at the wrong time. And who knows, maybe the head bit was optional.

If the meatballs weren't so delicious, I'd throw one at his face—to show my appreciation for his candor.

Whatever. My other questions shouldn't be as damaging to my self-esteem. Though who knows with this guy? Regardless, I ask, "Why not get a real girlfriend?"

"I don't do girlfriends."

I snort. "A charmer like you? What a loss for womankind."

I think I catch him wincing, but it must be either my imagination or one of those micro-expressions that are gone in an eyeblink. Have I gone overboard?

His expression now unreadable, he asks, "You realize I'm only answering your questions because I'm trying to be civil, right?"

This is him being civil? I'd hate to vex this guy.

"Fine," I say. "I withdraw my statement. Plenty of women would be happy to date you." Ever since *Fifty Shades of Grey*, masochism among women has surely been on the rise.

"I know you're being snide, but it's true. Many women want to date me... well, my money."

I nearly choke on my soup. "Am I supposed to feel bad for the poor *billionaire*? Most people would kill to have your gold-digger problem."

"And they'd regret it," he says, unblinking. "If the gold-diggers stop sniffing around me for the duration of our arrangement, that itself will almost make this all worth it."

"Almost... so that's not your main reason," I say. "What is?"

He nods at the papers by my elbow. "Sign the NDA, and I'll think about telling you."

Grr. "Why can't you just tell me now?"

He smirks. "Because I want the paperwork settled, and I bet you're curious enough to sign here and now."

"Maybe I am curious," I admit. "Would it get me killed if I were a cat?"

"If you were a cat, I'd probably die of allergies," he says, deadpan. "So it would be a murder-suicide situation."

Saguaro damn it. The proverbial cat died of wanting to know, and I feel like I might die if I don't find out right this second. And let's be honest, was I really going to get a lawyer?

I take the papers and skim them as thoroughly as I can considering my dyslexia and the fact that the closest I've gotten to law school is watching *Legally Blonde*. When I'm done, I think it's possible, even likely, that it all matches what Lucius has said. Then again, if it turns out I'm agreeing to do naughty pony play whenever he wishes, I won't be all that surprised either.

"Do you have a pen?" I ask grudgingly.

To his credit, he doesn't gloat. Instead, he simply pulls out a pen from his pocket and hands it to me.

Huh. The thing is heavy and very fancy-looking. Must be one of those Montblanc ones that cost thousands.

"I sign this and you tell me," I say. "None of that 'I'll think about it' bullshit."

"Deal." He sips his wine.

With a big sigh, I initial and sign the stupid papers, then push the stack toward him. "Talk."

He pockets the papers and the pen. "My grandmother has never been happy with my lack of dating. When she saw the article, she was so happy I didn't want to take it away from her."

I gape at him, waiting for a punchline.

He just finishes his soup and sips his wine.

He has a grandmother? I mean, obviously—I know he isn't a clone grown in an underground lab, and thus must have parents who also have parents and all that. He just doesn't strike me as someone who cares about making anyone else happy, grandmothers included.

"Oysters Rockefeller," the waitress/hostess says, startling me.

I wait for her to set down the plates and leave before whispering, "Is it me, or did she appear out of nowhere?"

Lucius flashes his dimple. "The staff in this restaurant attend ninja school."

Grinning, I taste the new entree—and this time, a moan does escape my lips.

Crap. Given how wide Lucius's eyes are, he heard that. Must change the topic, quickly. Thankfully, that part is easy. "Let's discuss the logistics of our fake relationship."

He scans the empty restaurant. "Given the ninja staff and all that, how about we just call it 'our relationship' going forward?"

"Hmm. That might be confusing. We need a word —and it can be a secret one—for when we want to emphasize the fakeness of it all."

"If you insist." He thinks about it for a beat. "How about *fartlek*?"

I suppress a groan. "Do we need to bring bodily functions into it?"

His lips flatten. "Don't be a child. *Fartlek* means 'speed play' in Swedish. It's a type of workout that's similar to interval training—you run fast, then you run slow, then fast again."

I roll my eyes. "I take it you like to fartlek?" Maybe after consuming large quantities of legumes?

"Sure. Fartlek strengthens willpower and endurance."

Endurance? Should I tell him that's not something we need for our fake relationship—sorry, our *fartlek*? Fighting a grin, I say, "Okay, what are our next steps... for the fartlek?"

He decimates an oyster as he considers my question. "How about we get to know each other?"

"Each other? I thought you knew all about me from your snooping."

He shakes his head. "I know useless information, like your credit score. I need to know things a boyfriend would know... especially what Gram thinks a boyfriend would know."

"Such as?"

He runs a hand through his hair, disheveling the

thick strands in a strangely adorable way. "I don't know. I don't do girlfriends."

I grab another oyster. "So... I'm to teach you how to do a girlfriend?"

He frowns. "There is no doing you, contractually." He pauses. "Having said that, Gram isn't good with boundaries, so why don't we start there." He looks me in the eyes. "What do you like?"

I flush, my mind returning to all my inappropriate fantasies. "Umm..." I know he doesn't mean what it sounds like, but—

"Sexually," he clarifies.

I drop the oyster.

Chapter 13

Lucius

SHE'S AGAIN DELIGHTFULLY PINK. Is she a prude? She didn't seem like one until now. Either way, I need her to answer. For Gram, not for myself.

"What do you like?" I repeat. "In bed."

"I guess..." She flushes brighter. "Kissing. Yeah, I like kissing."

I wave my hand. "You and every other woman. What else?"

"Umm... massages."

"Any specific types? Swedish, Shiatsu, Thai?"

"Foot," she squeaks. Even the tips of her ears are delectably red now.

"Foot?" My own blood rushes to my face, then takes a swift southern turn. I'm pretty sure she did say 'foot,' and now I'm hard.

She holds her wine glass as if it were Captain America's shield. "What's wrong with foot massages?"

"Nothing," I say quickly. "At all."

"You're not acting like it's nothing." She takes a careful sip of her wine.

Just in case, I hide my raging erection with a napkin. "It's just a coincidence, that's all."

Oops. She spit-takes the wine. "You also like getting foot massages?"

The fucking napkin is tenting, so I banish the look of her glorious feet from my brain and keep my face dispassionate as I say, "Not getting... giving."

Now her face turns even pinker, like a very girly flamingo.

This was clearly a bad idea. "I think we've covered this topic sufficiently. We—"

I spot what's-her-name with a tray and stop talking.

"Matcha panna cotta," she announces and plops a tiny plate in front of each of us.

Juno is either happy about getting dessert, or— more likely—glad the get-to-know-what-you-like conversation is over.

When we're alone again, I finish my earlier thought. "We have enough to satisfy my grandmother."

Juno grabs a dessert spoon. "Yeah. Learning her grandson's interest in feet is the kind of TMI that's going to make any grandmother regret asking."

Not *my* grandmother, but I don't tell Juno that.

She attacks the panna cotta and fucking moans, *again*—which doesn't help my cock stand down in the slightest.

"Do you think people will believe us?" she asks when she's done chewing.

I arch an eyebrow. "Believe the fartlek?"

She nods.

"Why wouldn't they?"

She doesn't meet my gaze. "You're you. I'm me. Why would they?"

I dip my spoon into the green dessert. "Could you be *more* vague?"

She sighs. "For starters, I'm a moneyless nobody."

"I have so much money most people are moneyless nobodies in comparison." I taste the dessert. It's not exactly moan-worthy but very good.

"So modest," Juno says with another eyeroll. "What I mean is, you should be with someone of the upper class. The kind of people that—"

"I hate," I say. "Snobs, all of them. *I* wasn't born with a silver spoon in my mouth."

She looks at her spoon, frowning. "Now that you mention it... Are these little spoons made of gold?"

I nod. "The chef insisted. Makes a big difference to the taste, especially for ice cream. Other options allegedly add a metallic aftertaste."

She stares at me, then slowly shakes her head. "If only I could have your problems for one day."

I scoff. "I'm not sure you'd cope."

She gives me a withering look. "How about we get back to business?"

"And what's that?"

"Something that will help sell the fartlek."

Makes sense. "Like what?"

She jabs the dessert with her spoon. "I don't know. This was your idea."

I eat another spoonful, but nothing comes to mind. "What do people talk about when they date?"

She shrugs. "Previous relationships?"

"That's easy," I say. "I haven't had any."

Juno's jaw hinges open. "None? Ever? Not even in high school or college?"

Women weren't interested in me before I made my first few million, but I'm not about to tell her that. Instead, I snap, "Why would I need a relationship? If it's for sex, I can get that whenever I want."

All that requires these days is some jewelry, but those one- or two-night flings are hardly "relationships."

At my sharp tone, she draws back. "Okay, whatever. But during our charade, you're going to abstain from sex with others, right?"

Interesting. "Jealous?" I ask, cocking my head.

"Yeah, right. I just don't want the gossip mags making me look like a fool."

"I'll abstain if you do." As the words leave my lips, I realize I like this idea *a lot.* So much so I'll have to berate my lawyer for not suggesting it.

"Deal," she says. "Want to write that into the contract?"

I get my pen out and write an addendum by hand.

Juno doesn't realize this, but I loathe such manual labor. Typing is way more efficient. However, this is important enough to lock it down here and now.

I wait until she initials the page, and then I surprise myself by genuinely wanting to know something I never thought I would.

"What about *your* relationships?"

Chapter 14

Juno

I PUSH the papers and the pen back to him with a jerky motion—a compromise, considering I feel like tossing them at his face. "I had one very long relationship. It ended eleven months ago."

I'm surprised this info wasn't discovered in his snooping. Unless it was, but he's forgotten already. It's not like he cares one iota about my life.

"Why did it end?" he asks, and manages to sound like he gives a shit.

"It just ran its course," I say.

No way am I rehashing the deets with someone I've just met, especially since he might already have everything in his dossier. Then again, how would Lucius's security team know that Jason called me stupid as he broke up with me? At most, they might've sussed out that I was with Jason all through his med school and residency, supporting his ambitions for years—and that in a horrible cliché, he broke up with me as soon as he became a full-fledged doctor.

Lucius is regarding me skeptically. "I'm not an expert, but I don't believe those things just run their course, for no reason."

"You want a reason?" To calm myself, I finish my dessert, even though it tastes like sawdust now. "Men are assholes, and our relationship turned out to be a fartlek-ing fartlek."

Lucius blinks, then extends his hand, as if to put his palm over mine. Only at the last second, he jerks it away. Then again, maybe I've imagined the whole thing. Or misunderstood. Maybe he was going to choke me to put me out of my misery.

"Anyway." I pointedly put down the little golden spoon. "Was this the last course?"

He also puts his spoon down. "That's up to us."

I rub my belly. "Donezo. What's next for our fartlek?"

"You'll accompany me to a boring fundraiser."

I snort. "Wow. You're selling that so well."

"I'm paying you enough to go even if you don't like it." He pockets his precious papers. "And who knows? You might end up having a good time, like the other meatsacks."

Meatsacks? Do I even want to know? Nah. Instead, I ask, "When is it?"

"Tomorrow."

"What's the dress code?" I look down frantically to make sure I didn't stain my outfit.

He makes a dismissive gesture. "The clothes will be provided."

Money *and* new clothes? I could get used to this. "Sounds like we're going to a fundraiser."

He pulls out a stack of hundreds and tosses a few on the table. "Let me take you home."

I gape at the money. "I thought this was your restaurant. Why do you need to pay?"

"I don't," he says. "That's a tip for what's-her-name." He points at the hostess/waitress.

He strides out, without so much as a thank-you or goodbye.

"Thanks. Everything was wonderful," I tell her, then hurry after Lucius.

When we get to the door, he stops, and I nearly crash into him.

"Do you need to use the bathroom before we go?" he asks.

I narrow my eyes at him. "Are you breaking our pact already?"

"How? I was just... Never mind." He approaches the limo and opens the door for me.

I get inside, but instead of joining me, he closes the door.

Huh. I guess I'm riding home by myself—and I haven't earned a goodbye either.

Chapter 15

Juno

As THE LIMO takes me home, all I can think about is how date-like what just happened was, especially for a business meeting—which is what it really was. The out-of-this-world food, the getting to know each other, the—let's be honest—attractive man I was with. Hell, Lucius even seemed somewhat less horrible. Some of the time, anyway. There were a few moments when he seemed downright likeable.

Wait. No. What the hell am I thinking? Finding Lucius likeable is like petting a wild raccoon without a rabies shot—too risky. To him, this is just a transaction, that's all. What we're about to do is as fake as the wax celebs at Madame Tussauds, and confusing it for an actual relationship would be foolish.

After what happened with Jason, I'm not looking to be in a real relationship, but if I were, it wouldn't be with a prickly asshole like Lucius, who—despite what he said about not being born with a silver spoon in his mouth—probably thinks of me as uneducated white trash.

The limo stops.

I thank Elijah and rush home. Once inside, I start to pace as I go over the whole situation.

The more I think about it, the more I realize how huge of a deal this is. For starters, I'll finally be able go to college. Or at least I can fund it now. I still need to apply—and acceptance is something I'm definitely worried about.

What I need right now is to share this whole crazy thing with someone—ideally, Pearl—but the stupid NDA is in the way.

Think of the devil. Pearl is calling me. Of course she is. She was here when Elijah stopped by.

Shit. The NDA means I'll have to lie to her. On the bright side, if Pearl buys the idea of me and Lucius dating, the rest of the world will too.

I accept the call.

"Dish," Pearl hisses instead of a hello.

I take a deep breath. "He told me he likes me."

The squealing sound that comes from Pearl's end of the phone is worrying. It's probably my friend producing the noise, but it could also be that she stepped on her cat's tail.

"Details," she demands when the sound subsides. "All of them."

"So... you know the article?"

"The one *I* showed *you*?"

Ah, right. "Turns out, the reason it was written was because of the adoring way Lucius looked at me when we exited the building. I didn't notice, but the journalists did, so he took me out to apologize… and to see if I liked him back."

"Tell me you do like him back," Pearl whispers.

I theatrically clear my throat. "You've seen his picture, right?"

The cat-tail shriek is back, this time with some stuck-pig undertones to it. "You're going to marry him! I can tell."

Marry him? It's a good thing she's not a witch because that fate sounds like it could be a curse.

"We haven't even had an official date yet," I say with exasperation. "Today doesn't count."

"Boo. And I'm guessing you haven't tapped that yet either? It takes six dates before you give up the goods, right? Or is it seven?"

"That is just a set of coincidences."

She lists my exes and the details of the sixth dates that led to sex, in great detail. Damn. I should be more careful when I tell her things, as she never forgets, like a gossip elephant.

"I think someone has just lost her confidante privileges," I say, playing up the genuine annoyance I feel.

"No. Wait. Sorry. Sleep with him whenever you want, but tell me all about it."

Time for the knockout punch. "Actually, hon, I have bad news in that department."

"No," she shouts. "Don't tell me he's asking you for an NDA."

Huh. "How did you know?"

"Because he's a fucking billionaire, and I've read *Fifty Shades*. But I can't *not* know. Can't you have him make an exception for me?"

"I tried," I say. "He said no... at least for now. Eventually, if things work out, who knows."

"No!" she screams, sounding like Darth Vader at the end of *Revenge of the Sith*. "Did you sign that shit already?"

"Not yet, or else I wouldn't have been able to tell you what I have."

"In that case, I need some juicy details, or else."

I scratch the back of my head. "I think he really likes my feet." That's not a complete lie, I don't think.

"O! M! G! You lucky fucking duckie. You'll get all the foot rubs you want!"

Thank goodness I've never told Pearl that foot rubs turn me on, or else she'd freak out so much someone would need to perform an exorcism.

"I have to take you out," she says urgently. "We'll get pedis, buy you an ankle bracelet, a toe ring, some open-toed shoes—"

"Sure," I say, because I know when resistance is futile. "How about later today?"

It might actually be nice to have my feet looking good for the next time I meet Lucius.

Pearl tells me what time she'll come and hangs up.

I face El Duderino. Since the NDA doesn't cover conversations with cactuses (at least I hope not), I tell *him* what really happened, in detail.

Dude. That's so metal. So what if this Lucius dude is a sucky dude? You're basically getting paid for eating nice grub.

I sigh.

Maybe it won't be so bad. For now, I'll focus on the best part: the possibility of a Botany degree.

Opening my laptop, I navigate to a folder with pre-prepared bookmarks and review the application requirements for the University of California-Irvine, California State Polytechnic University, and a few other colleges nearby that have a Botany program.

Then something hits me. Originally, I wanted to go to a local school because I couldn't afford to quit my business. Now, though, given how much money I'm going to get for the fartlek, I *could* consider going out of state.

With that in mind, I eagerly research and book-mark the most promising colleges. Given my B-minus high school grade average, I don't hold my breath when it comes to fancy places like Harvard and Cornell, but some state schools with very good Botany programs might be within my reach, like the University of Florida or Washington University.

The more I look into their application require-ments, though, the more I realize that my high school average might not be enough for them either. Which sucks, considering that it took me *a lot* of effort to get there with my dyslexia. No-social-life level of effort.

I sigh again. Hopefully, my essay will sway the admission officers, along with the fact that I run my own business. It's an extracurricular of sorts.

By the time Pearl texts me to let me know that she's downstairs and it's "shopping time," my eyes are blurry from staring at the screen for so long.

I close the laptop and face El Duderino.

"I guess it's time I go get accoutrements for my feet."

Chapter 16

Lucius

As always after a big meal, I hack my biology by taking a walk to improve my blood sugar levels, decrease stress, and aid sleep. Since this is Malibu and I have a private beach nearby, that is where I go.

Halfway to my destination, my phone rings.

It's Eidith.

I take the call and listen to a couple of updates absentmindedly.

"That's all I've got," she says, indicating the updates are over.

Yet she doesn't hang up.

That's odd, so I ask, "You sure there isn't something else?"

"Well... it's about tomorrow."

I wish this were a video call, so I could glare at her if this is about what I think it is. "I haven't forgotten about it." Eidith has taken it upon herself to look after my reputation—whatever that is. In this case, though, even I know a no-show for a fundraiser would be a social faux pas.

"Wonderful," she says, her voice sounding odd. "Will you wear something nice?"

Since I don't have video, I let irritation seep into my voice. "A suit, tie, and dress shoes, as always."

Is this about that time I hurt my foot in the gym and wore sneakers to that meeting with—

"I'm sure you'll be your dashing self," she chirps. "I was just—"

"I have to go," I say, since I've just reached the beach entrance.

"See you tomorrow," she says, again sounding odd, and then hangs up.

I turn off my phone and walk onto the beach.

As my feet luxuriate in the warm sand, I can't help but reflect on my meeting with Juno. Particularly how it was much less annoying than my usual interactions— including phone conversations—with people. By a lot. Usually, I agree with Oscar Wilde who said, "People are quite dreadful. One's self is the only society possible." But in this case, I actually didn't want our joint meal to end.

Also—and it might've been my imagination—Juno was much nicer to me toward the end. Like maybe there was a vibe going on...

No. What am I thinking?

She acted nicer because of the prospect of getting

money—and therefore her dreams coming true. What we're about to do is completely fake, and I have to remember that at all times, no matter how tempting she might be.

Besides, I didn't lie to her when I said I don't do girlfriends. But if I did, I wouldn't choose someone who turns me on so much. The last thing I want is for biology to rule me, instead of the other way around.

My phone pings.

It's an email from Eidith marked as "High Priority."

Turns out she was able to set up a video call with the Florida landowner today, as I hoped.

Great.

I check in with Elijah and learn he's dropped off Juno and is already waiting for me by the beach entrance.

————

"So, do we have a deal?" I ask the landowner—a man who's got a decade on Gram while being mentally sharper than some young middle-management types I deal with at my company.

The weather-beaten skin around his pale eyes crinkles. "Call me old-fashioned, but I still like to meet face to face before making an important decision like this."

Face to face? I'm not known for being polite or anything, but even I know it would be in poor taste for me to ask someone of this guy's age to come to me. That means a trip to Florida. I consider it. Even though I've had surveyors examine the land, and I've seen everything I need via drones, it might not be a bad idea to take it all in with my own eyes too. Novus Rome is important enough.

"An in-person meeting sounds like a great idea," I say, then work out all the details with him.

Just as I end the video call, my iPhone rings.

It's Gram calling, so I pick up.

"Lucius, pumpkin, what's new on the dating front?" she asks.

Going straight for the jugular, huh? "I had a nice lunch with Juno," I say. "And tomorrow, we're going to a fundraiser together."

Speaking of that, I wonder if she's received her clothing? Maybe I should—

"When are you going to introduce us?" Gram asks.

I've thought about this already, and the longer I can postpone it, the better. Juno and I need some time to work out the kinks. To that end, I've prepared a devious stratagem worthy of Eidith.

"I meant to talk to you about that, Gram," I say. "When do *you* think it would be a good idea for her to meet you? Or for me to meet her folks?"

The line grows silent. I can almost visualize the thoughtful expression on my grandmother's face.

Eventually, she sighs. "As much as I want to see her soon, you don't want to rush this part of the relationship. For these young women, meeting the family is a big step, and we don't want to spook her."

Even though my scheme is working, I feel guilt instead of triumph. "Oh, Gram. I'm sure *you* wouldn't spook her."

"Let's not take that risk," Gram says firmly. "I've waited a long time for you to find someone. I can wait a bit longer."

Hmm. Does she think that if I lost Juno, I'd take another thirty-eight years to get a girlfriend?

"Do keep me up to speed on how things are progressing," she continues. "I'll decide when the time is right... unless *she* brings it up."

There. I've just bought myself plenty of time.

"How are you feeling?"

She chuckles. "Amazing. I don't know what it is, but my sugar and blood pressure are the lowest they've been, my back pain is nonexistent without any drugs, and even my bowel movement today was that of a twenty-year-old."

If all this is corroborated in her bodyguard's report and is sustainable, I might want to "date" Juno forever and ever.

"I should probably go," Gram says. "Aleksy is taking me to his favorite Polish restaurant."

"Okay, have fun," I say as I decide to raise the bodyguard's salary.

"Call me the morning after the fundraiser," Gram says. "And be sure to take pictures."

As she hangs up, I realize pictures are a good idea. In fact, I'll hire someone to take flattering ones. As a bonus, it'll make it hard for the paparazzi who waste their time stalking me to sell theirs. Who'll pay for something that's free?

An alarm catches my attention.

Ah. It's the time I carved out for myself to work on Novus Rome.

I smile. Outside of playing with my ferrets, this is as close as I get to fun leisure time.

I get onto my treadmill desk, wake my computer, and open the Novus Rome folder.

What do I want to focus on today? Should it be the contactless payment for the self-driving car squad? Road and street light sensors? The interconnected digital health system for the hospitals and doctors' offices? Free ultra-high-speed internet that will cover thousands of acres?

No. I'd better consider the new variable that is Florida.

There will now be gators in the lake of Central Park—so small dogs will need to be leashed. More importantly, since there has never been a documented case of a hurricane making landfall in California, I didn't plan for them, but now I have to.

As usual, I do my own deep dive into a problem before I hire experts in the field. This way, I can't be as easily misled toward an inferior solution.

In this case, after hours of research, I decide that

luck is on my side. The round houses that we're planning to build are not only earthquake resistant, energy efficient, and economical in terms of interior to exterior space, but they should also fare extremely well in a hurricane due to how their shape interacts with wind.

I hear my usual "go to sleep" alarm.

Time always flies when I plan Novus Rome.

Before forcing myself away from the screen, I check to make sure Juno's outfit and shoes were delivered.

Yes. I have the confirmation, as well as an itemized receipt, which I shock myself by examining. As if possessed, I check out all the items—underwear included—and picture what Juno will look like wearing them.

Fuck. I have to snap out of it, or else I might bring about the last thing I need.

Yet another Juno-themed wet dream.

Chapter 17

Juno

RIGHT AFTER BREAKFAST, I get to work on my first college application, starting with the University of Florida because their website mentions things like greenhouses, a herbarium, and the Ethnoecology Garden.

Once again, I thank saguaro for the awesome invention that is the personal computer. It makes life so much easier for someone with my condition because it can read things on the screen out loud, and in general has settings that make everything a lot easier for me to read. If only my public school hadn't forced me to deal with paper. Alas, Arnold Schwarzenegger in his role as the Governator hadn't yet launched his initiative for digital textbooks. If I'd had text-to-speech in high school, I might've graduated as valedictorian, which would've helped my college applications tremendously.

I work tirelessly, pausing only to have a quick chat with El Duderino.

Dude, make sure to list me as a referral. It will totally impress those admission dudes.

By lunch, I realize that filling out college applications is a longer process than I thought, even though I have all my prerequisite info ready, like my scores and letters of recommendation. I also have an essay template, but I end up having to make a bunch of changes to make it fit the questions UF wants answered.

I'm just finishing up the application when my doorbell rings.

Weird.

I'm not expecting anyone. Quite the opposite.

I open the door.

A gang of fashionably dressed people is on my doorstep.

"Who are you?" I ask a guy with a rainbow Mohawk.

"I'm here to do your hair," he says. He points at the lady next to him, whose outfit reminds me of a disco ball. "She's your makeup artist."

Stunned, I step back to let them in. This is clearly Lucius's doing. Should I be pleased or insulted?

I'm not given a chance to decide.

The Mohawk guy orders me to dress for the event so that his work isn't ruined later.

The crew barely give me privacy as I put on my

new digs, and then it turns out one of them is merely here to make sure I look good in my outfit and to adjust what's needed.

When I finally sit in the kitchen chair designated as "my spot," the motley crew descends on me like vultures on roadkill.

———

The medieval torture—sorry, makeover—goes on for a decade before my doorbell rings.

"Oh, no," Mohawk guy says. "We're out of time."

The disco ball lady examines my face the way I would a pot of fungus-gnat-infested soil. "I guess this will have to do."

I open the door, and my breath hitches as I take in Lucius. He looks extra hot, and I can't figure out why. I mean, the last time I saw him, he was also dressed in a bespoke suit with a tie, was clean-shaven, and so on.

"Did you get a haircut?" I blurt.

Mohawk gasps and rounds on Lucius. "You saw someone else?"

Lucius frowns. "No haircut. I merely put some gel in."

Mohawk looks shocked. I guess grooming his hair is not in Lucius's usual repertoire.

Lucius hands Mohawk and the rest of the gang enough cash to open a salon. "That will be all."

Clutching the money, the makeover team skedaddles.

Lucius lifts a small, turquoise-colored shopping bag he's holding. "I got you a little something."

At first glance, my brain thinks the bag says "tip any & co." But no, it's all one word before the &, and the P is an F. An epiphany strikes. That's "Tiffany & Co.," as in—

"I hope it goes with your outfit." Lucius reaches into the bag and pulls out a box that's the same turquoise color as the bag.

I gape as he opens the lid, revealing a necklace littered with enough of a girl's best friends to form a small town. "You got me jewelry?"

He takes the bling out. "Score one for your powers of observation."

Rendered speechless, I just stand there as he steps behind me and drapes the necklace around my neck.

Holy saguaro. His fingers brush my neck, sending zingers of pleasure to my nipples and beyond. "There you go," he murmurs, his breath warm on the top of my head. "Now you look the part."

Shaken, I step away from his proximity, face the mirror attached to the front door, and check myself out.

Yep. If the part I am playing is that of a billionaire's girlfriend, Lucius and his team deserve an Oscar for costume design.

"We should go," Lucius says. "But first, give me a tour of your place."

A tour? I turn around and examine my tiny studio apartment. Does he think there are hidden rooms or something? Or that it's a TARDIS situation where something is roomier than it looks?

With a snort, I gesture to my left. "That's the kitchen." I point at my Murphy bed that doubles as a couch when not in use. "That's the bedroom and the living room. And last, but by no means least, my cactus." I smile at El Duderino. "End of tour."

"Oh." He glances at the only other door in my place. "That doesn't lead to more rooms?"

"Only if you consider a bathroom a room," I say. "And yes, I splurged so my toilet isn't just sitting in the middle of everything."

He walks over to the bathroom door and peeks inside.

Crap. Did I leave any unmentionables lying around? Given how unruffled he looks when he closes the door, probably not.

"Let's go," he says and strides for the front door.

He holds the door for me on the way out and when we get to the limo—proving you can be rude and a gentleman in one infuriating package.

We sit opposite each other, and he offers me a drink.

Wow, really playing up the gentleman bit.

"Thanks," I say pointedly when he hands it to me, so that maybe he'll add the word to his vocabulary at some point.

We sip our drinks in awkward silence. Then he says, "What kind of dog are you?"

I nearly choke on my champagne. "What?" Is this a roundabout way of him calling me a bitch?

He sighs, like my reaction is super unreasonable. "If we were dogs instead of humans, what breed would you be?"

"Why?" I ask—which is only the tip of the iceberg as far as my questions go.

"It's just a get-to-know-each-other question."

I cock my head. "You sure?"

He pulls out his phone and shows me the screen. "I looked up a few online."

He prepped for this? I scan the list of questions. Wow. The one he chose wasn't actually the worst one. There are pearls like: "If you were invisible, who would you snoop on?" and "What smell do you consider the worst?"

I blow out a breath in exasperation. "If I *had* to play this stupid game, I guess I'd pick a Chihuahua."

He nods approvingly. "Yappy, tiny, and mean—that tracks."

Will I break a clause in our contract if I throw this champagne in his face? "I chose a Chihuahua because of the Chihuahuan Desert, home to the Mexican fire-barrel and Arizona rainbow cactuses."

He sips his drink. "It's actually cacti, not cactuses."

My hackles rise. Or is it hackli? Dyslexia or not, I know this one. "You'll find both spellings in the dictionary, so why have something be an exception when it doesn't need to be?"

In general, if the English language were more regular, I'd have an easier time reading.

Lucius glares at me. "What do you mean, 'exception?' Cactus is of Latin origin and has an 'us' at the end. It's stimulus and stimuli, not stimuluses. Bacillus and bacilli, not bacilluses. Locus and loci, not locuses."

I roll my eyes. "Is grammar nazi the plural of 'grammar nazus?'"

"That doesn't even make sense," he says.

"Neither does cacti."

He sighs. "Fine. You want the next question?"

"No. You never said what kind of a dog you are." Probably a pit bull, or some other breed famous for bad temperament.

"Rottweiler," he says proudly.

Huh. I was close. "Untrainable and bad-tempered? That totally tracks."

"Those are misconceptions," he says. "Rottweilers have served humans for two thousand years. They were used in Ancient Rome."

I scoff. "How about I choose the next get-to-know-you question?"

He starts to hand me his phone, but I shake my head. "A normal question."

He arches an eyebrow. "Normal? You? Sure. What is it?"

"What's your favorite color?" I ask.

No doubt black, like his soul.

He looks me in the eyes. "Honey."

"That's pretty vague," I say. "The color of honey varies based on the nectar of the plant the bees eat. Orange blossom honey is lighter, while avocado is a darker amber."

"Light amber," he says. "What's your favorite?"

"Green," I say without hesitation.

He nods. "What kind of an aspiring botanist would you be otherwise?"

Wait, how does he—? Oh, right, the dossier.

"My turn again," he says. "When it comes to pets, are you a dog person, a cat person, or a ferret person?"

"How many of your questions are dog related? No, scratch that, what kind of a person is a ferret person?"

"Me." A hint of a smile plucks at his lips. "I have three of them."

"Ferrets?" Should I tell him he seems more like a lizard guy? Or someone who owns a hairless cat named Mr. Bigglesworth?

"Is that your next get-to-know-you question?" he asks.

"Why not?"

He tells me about his mother saddling him with the ferrets and the useful factoid that Romans used them to hunt mice.

I cringe. "Do you have mice?" I'm not a fan of mice, rats, gophers, or ground squirrels. They all eat cactuses.

"No mice. Just ferrets."

Good. "What kind of movies do you like?" I ask.

"It's my turn to pose a question."

I groan. "Fine. Go for it."

"If you had to listen to the same music over and over, loudly, what would it be?"

"That one's easy as I do that anyway," I say. "Metallica."

His eyes widen. "You're not going to believe this." He picks up a remote and hands it to me. "Up the volume."

I do as he says, and the familiar riffs of *Enter Sandman* blast out of the speakers.

That's right. He was listening to them in the elevator. How could I forget? I lower the volume back down before the urge to headbang grows too strong. That would mess up my carefully crafted hairdo, and I have a feeling that if the Mohawk guy saw a picture of such an atrocity, he'd find me and shave my head.

"They're my favorite too," Lucius says. "I'm just surprised *you* like them."

I squeeze the stem of my glass tighter. "Why?"

"You look like you might like Justin Bieber," he says without a second of hesitation.

If violence isn't the answer to anything, why does it seem like I'd enjoy it so much? "And you look like you might like Ariana Grande."

"Touché." He straightens his tie. "How did you get into Metallica?"

I sip the champagne. "I was trying to find out what

music my cactus liked. Most of it was as expected—The Beach Boys and other surf rock. The surprising one was Metallica. After a while, I grew to like it too—Metallica, that is, not the surfer stuff."

He's staring at me like I've morphed into a prickly plant myself. "Your cactus?"

"Yeah. I introduced him to you during the 'tour.'"

He shakes his head. "I didn't realize how important *he* was to you. I would've paid closer attention."

"Next time, you should. No one who knows me would believe our fartlek if you were anti-cactus."

He nods. "I'll keep that in mind."

Is he mocking me? Maybe not. "How did *you* get into Metallica?" I ask.

"My mother is a huge fan, so I heard it a lot growing up." He sets down his glass, a bit too roughly. "She even claims she dated a member of the band, though translated from Mom speak, that probably means a one-night stand."

Wow. There's a lot to unpack there, but before I get the chance, the limo stops and Elijah does his magic-trick-style door-opening routine.

"Here we are," Elijah says when we come out.

"Here" happens to be the parking lot of California Science Center, a place I've been only once and so long ago that I barely remember anything except how cool the building looks on the outside.

To my absolute shock, Lucius grabs me by my hand.

116

Oh. My. Saguaro.

As he leads me inside, my palm feels like it's going to orgasm... and then maybe explode. I don't understand this reaction. At all.

Sure, his hand is big and warm and all, but I don't even like the guy.

Our destination is a hangar where the space shuttle Endeavour hangs. Someone set up big round tables under the shuttle, with flowers and fancy chairs and other ritzy stuff.

Lucius leads me to a table under the shuttle's left wing and pulls out one of the two remaining empty chairs.

Slightly overwhelmed, I sit and thank him.

A blond, extremely polished, and classically beautiful woman is sitting a couple of chairs over. She examines me with cold curiosity. The glittery, fancy surroundings seem to be her natural habitat, whereas I must stand out like a desert cactus in a swamp.

When Lucius sits down, she switches her attention to him—and I don't like the admiring expression on her face at all.

"Hi," I say to her with mock cheerfulness. "Looks like we're the only girls at the table."

The portly gentleman to my left chuckles.

The woman tears her gaze away from my date. "Hello. I don't believe we've been introduced."

Damn. I didn't realize it's possible to sound "old money," but she manages it perfectly.

Lucius gestures at her. "Juno, this is Eidith. She works for me."

Hmm. "For" is better than "under," I suppose.

"That's Eidith with an extra 'i,'" Eidith says.

Why add extra letters into words or names?

"Eidith, this is Juno, my girlfriend," Lucius continues.

Wow. As soon as she hears the g-word, Eidith's face goes through a kaleidoscope of expressions. Shock, disappointment, and incredulity are the start, followed by an essay-length opinion that boils down to:

Trash like this doesn't belong with someone as rich and successful as Lucius. Only a pure-bred member of the one percent does. Someone like, say, me, Eidith with an extra "i."

The most impressive part is how quickly all of that is gone, replaced with a smile that you could locate in a dictionary next to "cool politeness."

"It's very nice to meet you, Juno," Eidith says, sounding so earnest I almost wonder if I imagined her initial reaction.

"Nice to meet you too," I say.

A waiter approaches with a tray of drinks, so everyone grabs a glass.

"How did the two of you meet?" Eidith asks with seemingly genuine curiosity.

Crap. How could we not have prepared for something this basic?

"We got stuck in the elevator," Lucius says.

Huh. Going with the truth. Ballsy.

Eidith clutches her pearls. "During that basement fire?"

"Yep," I chime in. "I was cold, and he gave me his jacket."

"And then we hit it off," Lucius says.

Yeah, hits almost got thrown, that's for sure.

"A silver lining to a disaster," Eidith says and again sounds like she means it.

Seriously, have I misjudged her?

"Exactly," Lucius says. "When we got outside, the reporters must've picked up on our vibe, so they wrote an article about us. Haven't you seen it?"

Judging by the look on Eidith's face, she hasn't but thinks she was supposed to.

Before Lucius can lie more about our meeting, a horde of waiters arrives with trays of appetizers that they set on the table.

"Is this thing on?" says someone on the big stage—a celebrity whose name I can't recall.

As the room quiets down, the celeb says, "Thank you so much for showing up to support the children."

Children? I was wondering what this fundraiser was about.

As I listen, I grab myself a deviled egg and a cracker with caviar.

Turns out, we're here to support bringing technology to classrooms in the neighborhoods that desperately need it—a spooky coincidence given my musings about text-to-speech earlier today.

As I look from the stage back to my plate, I do a double take.

Most of my egg is missing, as is all of the caviar. Only the filling from the egg and the cracker remain.

What the hell?

I sneak a peek at the portly gentleman next to me. He's eating other appetizers. Besides, there are more eggs and caviar on the table, so why steal from my plate?

Maybe it was Eidith? She's so thin she could use extra food. But no. She's too many seats away to get away with it unnoticed.

Oh, well. I grab some more and watch my plate carefully. Nope. Despite this hanger being space-themed, there isn't a wormhole that just happens to connect my plate with another galaxy. Both chicken and fish eggs stay put—until I eat them.

"And now, we welcome everyone to the dance floor," the celeb says, and club music begins to blast.

Is Eidith looking at Lucius with hope in her eyes?

Oh, no, you don't. If anyone is dancing with my fake boyfriend, it's me.

As if reading my mind, Lucius lowers his lips to my ear and asks in a sexy whisper, "Would you like to dance?"

Chapter 18

Lucius

JUNO FLAPS her long lashes at me for a few seconds before she stands up. "Sure."

I lead her to the dance floor, where we join a few other couples. The song the DJ plays must be by Ariana Grande because it's a woman's voice and Juno grins like a loon as she tells me, "That's your favorite."

I'm not usually a fan of dancing, but seeing Juno move makes the chore surprisingly tolerable. It must be her bright smile. Or the sway of her rounded hips. Or the sparkle in her honey-colored eyes. Or it could be the fact that her fast-moving feet are difficult to ignore. Speaking of that, has she always had that ankle bracelet and toe ring?

I drag my gaze back to her face. She's wearing that same bright smile that captured me earlier. Suddenly, she pales and glances at someone to our left. Her smile evaporates, replaced with a deep frown.

"What is it?" I follow her gaze and see a boring couple: a shifty-looking man about my age and a woman who is clearly one of those annoying heiresses with a trust fund and enough entitled attitude to kill a horse.

"That's my ex," Juno says in a slightly choked voice. "With his new wife. The richer and smarter upgrade."

Richer? Who cares? Smarter? I highly doubt it. To give credit where credit is due, Juno's mind is razor sharp.

The shifty guy spots us, and for whatever reason, he seems to be looking more at me than at Juno as he drags his wife over to us.

What fresh hell is this?

"Juno," he screams over the music when they're close enough. "What are you doing here?"

"She's my date," I retort and try my best to project an attitude of "now leave us the fuck alone."

The guy looks on the verge of drooling. "You're Lucius Warren, right?"

As usual, I can tell what he's really saying, and it is: *You're that guy who can do something for me. Please be that guy. Pretty please.*

"That's him," the wife says, beaming. "I told you it's him."

"What are you doing here?" Juno demands.

The ex shrugs. "This cause is important to the wife."

Is it really the cause, or getting glammed up and mingling with the right people?

Juno looks just as skeptical as I feel. "Well," she says. "Nice bumping into you two."

Translation from polite speak:

It sucked ass, so go away.

"I heard you're soliciting doctors for a secret project," the ex says to me, beady eyes shining.

And there it is. *Can I please be on Project Novus Rome? Pretty please.*

"It's true," I say. "But why do you care? I'm looking for the *best* doctors."

Is it clear that I'm implying "and you're not one of them?" Yep. Based on the widening eyes of Juno and the guy's wife, the message gets through. The ex must get it as well, since he looks like he's considering throwing a punch.

I give him a look that says, *Yes, please. Great idea. Make coming to this shindig worth my time.*

Sadly, he chickens out. "We'd better let the two of you dance," the dipshit says to Juno. "Let's hug and—"

"Hug?" My hands ball into fists.

He takes a step back. "I'm a hugger."

Juno rolls her eyes but nods. "Always has been."

"I'm a puncher," I state. "Are we going to indulge our natures today?"

The ex turns on his heel and walks away. His wife huffs indignantly and follows.

"Caveman," Juno says to me, but the smile that tugs at the corners of her eyes betrays her.

I'd bet a million bucks she's glad her ex just looked like an ass.

"Let's resume the dance," I say.

She nods, and in that moment, the music changes to a slow song.

"This is our chance to show everyone this fartlek is real," I whisper into her ear.

"You're right." Her expression is unreadable as she steps closer. "Let's make them eat their hearts out." With that, she puts her forearms on my shoulders.

Fuck. Her nearness is intoxicating.

Then again, maybe I can use this as a chance to train myself to resist biological urges. I put my hands on her hips, pull her close, and start moving to the rhythm of the music.

Double fuck. We've barely started, and I'm already losing the battle against my body.

She just smells too delicious, and staring into the amber depths of her eyes is too hypnotizing.

Can she feel my raging erection?

Her Mona Lisa smile doesn't say one way or another.

She rises on tiptoes to reach my ear with her lips. "You're a good dancer."

"Am I?" My cock twitches at the warm puff of her breath, and my voice is much too husky as I say, "That's news to me."

She nods, looking up at me. "Where did you learn?"

I force myself to focus. "I sometimes dance with my grandmother."

She looks insultingly surprised. "You do?"

"Yeah. Why not? Is there something about me that says 'hates his grandmother?'"

She licks her lips maddeningly. "No. Sorry. I just didn't expect you to say that."

Damn it.

Her lips call to me, like those sirens that drown sailors.

I pull her closer, and she seems not to mind.

I lean down without meaning to, and she—

Fuck.

I freeze, looking to the side.

Is that what I think it is?

Yep. A furry creature is scurrying across the dance floor, holding a piece of deviled egg.

I must be imagining it.

I squint.

Nope.

That's Blackbeard, one of my ferrets.

Chapter 19

Juno

HOLY SAGUARO.

Lucius was about to kiss me.

And I think I might have let him.

Fortunately, he stopped, and the idea must really repulse him now—at least that's how I interpret his letting me go and staring under everyone's feet so intently.

"I'll be back," he says and starts making his way toward the stage.

Huh?

He grabs a microphone and shouts, "Everyone, freeze! Do not move an inch. My ferret has escaped onto the dance floor, and if anyone steps on him, I will personally step on you with all of my lawyers."

By saguaro's spines. Everyone indeed freezes, the music stops, and many things happen at once.

"Did he say *feral rat*?" my ex's new wife shouts and jumps onto the nearest chair.

I'm pretty sure he said "ferret," given that he owns ferrets and all. Regardless, at the word "rat," some woman shrieks like a banshee on crack, and a middle-aged man hops onto a chair, which promptly topples over. More shrieks ensue, and dozens of women flip up their skirts, like floosies in a western saloon. Others climb onto their chairs, and a few particularly adroit socialites end up on tables. Everyone else remains frozen—either in shock or due to Lucius's threat.

Out of the corner of my eye, I spot a furry shadow as it dives under a nearby empty table.

"There!" I shout for Lucius, then run for the—hopefully—ferret.

When I get to the table, there's no creature in sight, but I do see a piece of egg with ferret-sized bite marks in it.

So this is what happened to my caviar and egg appetizer. The ferret must've nabbed it.

Lucius hurries over. "Blackbeard!"

"He's not here," I yell back. He named his ferret Blackbeard? That's like *asking* the poor creature to cause trouble. Though maybe he named the ferret *after* he got to know him.

I frantically look around. Everyone who's not on a chair or a table is still frozen in place, looking under their feet in horror.

Then I see him. "Blackbeard is on the stage!"

Lucius must hear me because he sprints over there, just as I do the same.

Meanwhile, Blackbeard grabs the cable attached to the microphone with his teeth and gives it a tug.

The mic begins to tip over.

Oh, no.

What if it crushes the—

Whew.

The metal rod misses the ferret by an inch and hits the ground with a deafening screech that makes everyone slap their palms over their ears.

Unlike the humans, Blackbeard looks more intrigued than scared. He scurries over to the microphone, and judging by the ensuing crunching sounds, tries to eat it.

I run up the staircase leading to the stage, and Lucius does the same on the other side.

This is it.

We have the critter cornered.

We leap for him.

Our bodies collide. Lucius's hand lands on my boob, but the ferret escapes, clucking excitedly.

"Sorry," Lucius says, stumbling back. "That was an accident, I swear."

"No worries," I lie. My nipple is distinctly peaked where he touched me, and my breathing is more than a little unsteady—and not just from the ferret chase. "Let's get him."

We track Blackbeard to the other end of the room, where he stops and looks up at the space shuttle.

His thoughts aren't hard to read:

Argh! If I could get in there, I could be the first-ever space pirate. Aliens and Predators would shiver their timbers—whatever that means—and walk the space plank.

I move slowly, worried I'll be noticed. As I pass by a nearby table, I grab a deviled egg.

Behind the ferret, Lucius is also creeping closer, but without any bait.

When I'm ten feet away, the ferret looks right at me with a mischievous look in his eyes.

"Hey, little furball." I drop the egg between us. "Come get this juicy booty."

Pirates like booty, right?

Wait, why are people looking at my butt?

Whatever. The good news is that the bait idea works. Blackbeard scurries to the egg, glancing at me cautiously from time to time. What the poor ferret doesn't realize is that I'm a distraction.

Just as he swallows the egg, Lucius grabs him from behind.

"Time to take this one home," Lucius says, holding his little friend gently but firmly.

I follow the two of them to the limo.

Once we're inside, Lucius asks, "Do you mind if I take him home first?"

"Of course not," I say. "Can I hold him?"

Lucius gives Blackbeard a scratch that kind of makes me jealous. "Do you mind waiting until we get into the greenhouse? It's ferret proof... or so I thought."

My lips stretch into a smile. "How do you think he got out?"

Lucius lifts his shoulders. "I played with them before I left. So maybe he got into my jacket pocket?"

I touch the gorgeous necklace. "Did you have the Tiffany's bag with you?"

He gives Blackbeard a respectful glance. "You're right. He must've snuck inside that bag, then hid somewhere in this car."

I chuckle. "That's one nice thing about my cactus. He stays put."

Lucius pets his ferret's fur with a slight eyeroll. "Not as nice to the touch, though, your cactus."

"But he can produce life-giving oxygen, so it's a tradeoff."

Lucius doesn't look convinced, but thankfully, he changes the topic. "Do you want to keep playing the-get-to-know-you game?"

I sigh. "Sure. What was the next question on that genius list you dug up?"

Holding the ferret with one hand, he pulls out his phone with the other and gives it a brief glance. "Do you prefer party balloons or clowns?"

I wait for the punchline that never comes. Even the ferret is like, "How is that relevant?"

I blow out a breath. "Balloons, I guess. Clowns are

scary."

"They are now, but they weren't throughout history—which they have a lot of. Even in Ancient Rome, they had *stupidus*—a type of clown. I bet it was John Wayne Gacy and Pennywise from *It* that made clowns scary. Maybe the Joker too."

I consider it. "Nope. I didn't like clowns as a kid—without exposure to any serial killers or fictional evil clowns. I think it was about their weird outfits and makeup."

Lucius lifts Blackbeard to his face and rubs his stubbly-looking cheek against the ferret's fur. "What did you want to ask me?"

I gape at him. Am I hallucinating, or is this the least asshole-y thing I've ever seen any man do? I mean, cuteness-wise, this is right up there with a dude cuddling a baby, and Lucius must do this regularly because Blackbeard seems to like it. The ferret closes his eyes in evident pleasure. If he were a cat, I bet he'd purr.

This is not what I would've expected from Lucius. At all.

I pull my scrambled brains together. "What's your favorite movie?"

He scoffs. "How is this question better than the ones on the list you've been whining about?"

Ah, the dickish Lucius is back... or he never left. "I bet I could learn a lot about you from the answer."

"Fine," he says. "*Gladiator*. What does that tell you?"

I grin. "That we have something in common. I love that movie. It also tells me that, like me, you think Russell Crowe is hot. Right?"

Was that a hint of a smile? "No," Lucius says. "But he did give a great performance, and the film is the best of all the ones I've seen depicting Rome."

Boom. A collection of his other answers flits through my brain, along with those stupid elevator buttons. "You're *really* into Ancient Rome, huh?"

"And you're really into cactuses. So what?"

I stick my tongue out—a gesture the ferret instantly parrots before taking it further by licking Lucius's cheek. "Just shows you how much I've learned about you thanks to this one question."

Lucius uses his shoulder to wipe ferret saliva from his face. "You win. I'll be asking future dates about their favorite movie. Happy now?"

No. Not at all. I hate the idea of him on future dates... with other people, that is. "Why Rome?" I ask, eager to mask my irrational reaction.

He presses the ferret to his chest as if the little creature were a baby. "My mom took me there when she was into it. For her, it turned out to be yet another phase. For me, it stuck."

There seems to be something unspoken here, especially considering that suggestion that his mom had a one-night stand with one of the Metallica members.

"Are you and your mom close?" I ask gently.

His lips grow tight. "Not anymore."

"Oh?" is all I trust myself to reply with.

His steel-colored eyes turn hard. "She left me to travel the world when I was eight. Being a mother was just another phase for her. My grandmother raised me. But enough about me. Why do you like cacti so much?"

I get the feeling I'd better leave the issue of his mom alone. "Why wouldn't I like cactuses?"

"Because you'd regret touching one?"

Some unkind words are on the tip of my tongue, but given what he's just shared about his mother, I swallow them. "You're wrong. Cactuses are awesome. They're tough. They thrive where other plants wouldn't even dare to grow. They have hidden depths to them. You may see a few inches of a cactus above ground, but its roots can be seven feet deep. Despite their spines, when the conditions are right, cactuses have the most beautiful blooms. And they—"

The limo stops in front of tall, wrought-iron gates.

"Almost home," Lucius says as the gates slide apart, giving me a glimpse of a sprawling mansion that looks like a modern art museum.

I whistle. "Did you steal the designs for the Getty Center?"

He tightens his hold on the suddenly-more-excited Blackbeard. "Both the Getty Center and the Getty Villa inspired my home."

Makes sense. J. Paul Getty was a billionaire in the previous century, so why not use him as a role model?

The limo traverses the gorgeous courtyard until it stops next to a large domed building. "In there," Lucius says as Elijah opens the door. "I think you'll like the greenhouse."

We exit, and as soon as we step through the door into said greenhouse, Blackbeard starts barking—and a chorus of barks echoes back.

In a blur of fur, two more ferrets arrive and start goofing around.

"Were you worried about Blackbeard?" Lucius asks them, gently setting the furry creature on the ground.

In reply, one ferret nibbles on Blackbeard's butt, the other on Lucius's shoe. Then the ferrets begin chasing each other merrily.

"That's Caligula and Malfoy." Lucius points to each ferret in turn. There's a distinct note of fatherly pride in his voice.

"Great names. You've got a pirate, an insane tyrant, and a pure-blooded Slytherin."

Also... should I mention that Draco Malfoy's dad was named Lucius?

Nah. I'm sure he knows.

Lucius chuckles. "I've toyed with the idea of getting one more. If I do, I'll call that one Fluffy."

I grin. "And it will turn out to be the evilest one."

Lucius's eyes linger on my face. "Want to check out the rest of the greenhouse?"

I do, and he leads me though the giant space. Every corner has a litter box—presumably for the ferrets. Personally, I'm more intrigued by the veritable cornucopia of plant species, like kalanchoe, peperomia, snake and spider plants, moth orchid—the list goes on and on.

When we return to the entrance, Lucius says, "If you liked this, there's something you have to see in the gardens outside."

He has gardens too? I fight the urge to jump up and down. "Yes, please."

He lets me go first, then closes the door carefully, making sure the ferrets stay behind.

I follow him through rows of yarrows, bearberries, and checkerblooms until we reach our destination.

It's a cactus garden.

I gasp in awe.

Majestic golden barrel cactus. Magnificent prickly pear. Beautiful dollar cactus. And on and on.

"Look at you, handsome creatures," I croon as I approach each one, forgetting for a second where I am.

Lucius falls into step next to me. "So you don't just play Metallica to cacti? You converse with them as well?"

"Cactuses," I say. "And yes, I do. Do you have a problem with that?"

He regards me seriously. "I think it's cute."

My stomach feels fluttery, like a cactus flower being pollinated by a hummingbird.

I dampen my dry lips. "Is this another inspiration from the Getty Center?"

He cocks his head. "How so?"

I blink at him. "You've never seen the cactus garden there? That's the most beautiful spot in all of LA." I turn to his cactuses. "Or the second most."

He examines his cactuses as if for the first time. "I think I'll hire the garden designer I used for my home to help with Novus Rome."

I reluctantly drag my gaze away from the majestic beings that are his cactuses. "Novus Rome?"

His eyes widen. "I haven't told you about Novus Rome?"

"Nope."

"Come, let me give you a tour, and I'll explain."

So he does, and as far as I can understand, Novus Rome will be a futuristic smart city built and run exactly to Lucius's meticulous specifications. He doesn't explain why he wants this, but I figure it's because it's the ultimate power trip. I've always suspected that once you're rich enough, you start wanting to play God.

During the explanation, I also get to see Lucius's so-called home—a ridiculous display of wealth made out of concrete and glass. Each room is labeled with a Latin inscription, which Lucius translates as the Sun Room, the Atrium, and so on. Unsurprisingly, there are many Gallery Rooms dedicated to all things Rome. They remind me of wings in a natural history museum. Slightly more interesting is the Metallica Room, where Lucius displays paraphernalia that belonged to the band, most of it signed. Whenever I ask, it turns out the item in question was bought at some auction for a truly obscene price.

He stops talking when we reach a tall set of doors, with a word etched into one that my brain perceives as "Cumbilubecube." Lucius reads it as *Cubiculum*, which doesn't make that much more sense, but whatever.

"Where will you build Novus Rome?" I ask. "On a deserted island?"

He stops and faces me. "On a peninsula. You might have heard of the place. It's called Florida."

I snort. "Oranges and sunshine?"

"That's the one. I'm buying an epic plot of land not far from Gainesville."

"Jinx! I just applied to the University of Florida, which is in Gainesville."

He smiles faintly. "Double jinx then—I'm flying over there tomorrow."

"You are?" I find it hard to keep the jealousy out of my voice.

His eyes glimmer. "Why don't you join me?"

I blink at him. "Join you on a work trip?"

"Why not?"

"Because I don't have a plane ticket, for starters."

He waves that away. "We'd be flying on my jet."

Of course he has a private jet. It comes standard with this mansion.

"I don't want to intrude." It's hard to sound like I mean it because I absolutely, totally would love to fly on a private jet to check out the UF campus.

"You wouldn't be intruding," he says. "It would give us a chance to get to know each other better. I rarely do anything productive when I fly, so it would work out perfectly."

"So... I'm to be your in-flight entertainment." Crap. Did that sound dirty?

He looks at me with a strange expression. "Is that a yes?"

"Sure." I clear my suddenly dry throat. "Let's continue the tour?" I nod at the Cubiculum.

"I'm not sure if it's proper for us to go in there," he says with a frown. "That's my bedroom."

"By golly." I clutch the diamond necklace theatrically. "And without a chaperone? Unthinkable."

He grumbles something under his breath, then gestures at a room we haven't visited yet. "How about we go to the Study?"

"Sure. What's after that—the Wine Cellar? Or the Lounge? The Vault, maybe?"

"If you wish," he says, his expression deadpan. "I'm not a huge wine connoisseur, so my cellar is pretty small."

Yeah, right. Probably bigger than my whole apartment.

As we enter the Study, I realize it might be the most modest room in the whole place. I see a couch, a bookshelf, a pretty rug, and a pillar topped with a beautiful cameo-glass-embroidered vase—likely from Ancient Rome. It appears to be the only crazy-expensive thing in the room... unless all the books are first editions signed by the authors. Or the legs of the couch are made of diamonds. Or the rug is made of gold thread, then painted over.

I look around as I pointedly furrow my eyebrows. "Where is the room with the pool?"

He frowns. "You saw the pool."

"No, the one filled with gold that you swim in. You know, like Scrooge McDuck?"

He steps toward me, eyes gleaming with either laughter or mischief. "Did you know that Caligula— the historical figure, not my ferret—used to do something like that? He'd put gold on the ground and wade through it, or walk over it with bare feet." He glances at my feet as he says this, and if the idea is to channel that historical figure famous for an insatiable libido, he does it eerily well.

My breath quickening, I take a step back—and trip over the edge of the rug.

Crap!

I flail my arms, trying to grab onto something to break my fall. My hand smacks into the vase, sending it flying—but doing nothing to stop my butt from its inevitable collision with the floor.

Except it's not so inevitable.

Right before my coccyx kisses the hard marble, powerful hands catch me, and I find myself looking into Lucius's concerned face—even as a loud crash reaches my ears.

Oh, shit. The vase.

Judging by the sound, it's in pieces.

"I've got you," Lucius murmurs, relief evident in his voice.

"But not the vase," I gasp, looping my arms around his strong neck. Speaking in his embrace is surprisingly difficult, especially since he's still holding me in a semi-horizontal position, as if dipping me in tango.

"Don't worry about that," he says without a second of hesitation. For some reason, he doesn't seem to be in a hurry to set me upright and release me.

I moisten my lips. "But... was it expensive?"

His metallic eyes never leave mine, the gleam in them hypnotizing. "Priceless."

Gulp. I'm not sure if it's the fall or the guilt, but I feel kind of floaty. Am I on the verge of fainting?

"Are you okay?" he asks, no doubt because my body has slackened in his arms.

I stare at him as I try to think of an answer. On the one hand, his muscular arm cradling my back feels amazing. On the other, I feel terrible about the ancient artifact that I ruined—even if he doesn't seem to care about that. Since I can't trust myself not to babble, I reply with an abridged version—a breathy "I'm fine."

He finally moves to stand me upright, and I become hyperaware of the trajectory of our lips. Specifically, the minor corrections I need to make to put them on a collision course. They're only a few inches apart. Now three inches, two, one... liftoff.

By the space saguaro, NASA would be proud of me.

Like a shuttle docking with a space station, our lips lock. Heat rushes through me, like a solar flare, and our tongues dance, like a planet and its moon. If mouths could see, mine would be blissfully admiring stars, nebulas, and distant galaxies. Endorphins explode in my brain like supernovas, and I feel a dampness between my legs, like... err ...something wet in space.

I arch against him, and something hard presses into my stomach.

His erection.

Oh, shit. What are we doing?

I let go of his neck, staggering back—and it's a miracle I don't end up on my ass after all. Or break another priceless something.

Panting, I touch my lips, staring at him. "I... I'm sorry."

The edges of his cheekbones are painted with dark color, and his breathing seems equally uneven. Then, even as I watch, a hard mask drops in place over his features. "I kissed *you*," he says harshly. "Shouldn't *I* be sorry?"

He did? I thought I kissed him. Whatever.

Whoever started it, we sure went at it with an enthusiasm that breaks every rule we've agreed upon.

"I think I should go." I look around stupidly—as though an exit from the mansion will magically materialize in this room.

"Understood." He rings a bell hanging on the wall.

I blink as Elijah appears almost instantly. Apparently, opening limo doors is only one of his mythical butlery skills.

"Take Juno home," Lucius says imperiously.

With a curt nod, Elijah gestures for me to proceed to the door.

I follow him, my steps zombie-like, and only when I reach the limo do I realize that I never said goodbye to Lucius.

He didn't say it to me either, though in his defense (if it could be called a defense), he's a rude bastard.

As the car starts moving, the enormity of what's just happened slams into me, like a bull into an inexperienced matador.

Lucius and I kissed.

And I liked it.

More than liked it.

But he didn't. Or did he? There was an erection...

But then why kick me out?

Did he kick me out?

Either way, what was I thinking? I clearly wasn't. That's what happens when you let ovaries take over for the brain. Is our deal off now? Have I messed up our arrangement?

The questions swarm my neurons all the way home and as I go through my evening routine, I come up with exactly zero answers.

It's not until I'm falling asleep that one more question rises to the surface.

Am I still going to Florida tomorrow?

Chapter 20

Lucius

As soon as Juno leaves, I want to punch myself in the dick—the culprit for this fiasco.

Hmm. A variation on that might not be the worst idea. I slam and lock the door to my bedroom before I fist my cock—eager to release the sexual energy before something in my balls explodes.

Cleaning up after, I label what happened as what it was: my worst loss to biology, ever. And it's not Juno's fault—she can't help being hot as hell. But it was *my* idiotic idea to get her dressed up and made up on top of that, as though I wanted to challenge my self-control.

Well, I fucking failed. Now she's probably going to flake on the whole fartlek, even before I get the chance to parade her in front of Gram.

Maybe it's for the best. Still, a part of me is disappointed that she'll be out of my life—a part that's certifiable, no doubt.

As usual for me, I arrive at a decision in a heartbeat.

I will not call or text her to check where we stand. I'm just going to send Elijah with the car for her tomorrow morning, like nothing has changed. If she refuses to go, I'll think of another solution.

With that, I give in to biology once again by wasting potentially productive time on sleep.

———

I'm on my laptop in my stationary jet when a text from Elijah arrives.

She got into the car.

The rush of relief I feel is illogical, but I don't want to examine it too closely—opting to focus on work instead, since as soon as the engines start roaring, I'll have a hard time concentrating, even with noise-canceling headphones on. Not to mention, Juno's arrival might also mess with my concentration.

Hell, she's not even here yet and she's doing it.

———

Someone clears her throat.

I look up from my laptop.

Yep.

There she is.

Juno.

145

She's dressed a lot more casually today, in jeans, a T-shirt, and sandals—yet she still somehow manages to look sexy.

Distractingly so.

"Hello." I shut my laptop—a courtesy I've shown to only a select few people.

She puts her hands on her hips. "Is that all you have to say to me?"

I stash the laptop under my seat. "Hello... how are you?"

Her honey eyes gleam like bee stings. "So that's how you want to play it?" She then smiles sweetly at me, and in a voice that reminds me of the way she talks to plants, she says, "I'm great, darling. How are you?"

I sigh. "Is this about what happened yesterday?"

"Oh?" she asks in that same honey-laced tone. "What happened yesterday?"

"We were practicing for our roles. Obviously." There. A perfect out.

She stares at me for a couple of beats, and I can't tell if she's relieved or upset. Eidith would be able to figure it out, but I'm having trouble. I would ask, but even I know that some things are better left unsaid.

Finally, Juno blinks, breaking our eye contact, and asks in her normal voice, "Where can I sit?"

Chapter 21

Juno

LUCIUS GESTURES at the spacious seat opposite him, so I head over there.

This morning was a rollercoaster ride. I still can't believe he sent his butler for me like nothing's happened. But I guess it makes sense if he considers what went down yesterday as some sort of PDA practice.

By saguaro's needles, I've never felt this conflicted. I should be relieved that the kiss wasn't anything, but I can't help an irrational feeling of disappointment. I must've wanted it be real. Or some crazy part of me wanted it.

I plop gracelessly into the leather seat, and it feels like a cloud. Ignoring Lucius for the moment, I scan the luxurious interior of the jet.

Damn.

Having passed by first-class sections on regular

planes, I can compare this to them, and it's like a five-star hotel versus a rat-infested hovel.

"If you want a massage, just press this button." Lucius points at a controller next to his elbow.

Intrigued, I do so.

My chair comes to life. It leans me back, and the armrests and footrest open up, like three hungry gators.

"If you want an arm and/or foot massage, stick the appropriate appendages in there," Lucius explains.

At the mention of a foot massage, I flush. Does he remember what I said that time? Probably—I still recall him saying he likes to give them...

Whatever. To satiate my curiosity, I stick my arms into the arm sections, and then, after a slight hesitation, I kick off my sandals and put my feet into the bottom part.

Hmm. Did Lucius's gaze linger on my feet a moment too long? If so, why? Was I supposed to wear socks... or does it have to do with that whole foot-massage convo—

Wow. The massage begins, and it's amazing. Maybe too amazing—a moan is on the verge of escaping my lips.

"How do I turn this off?" I ask urgently.

Lucius leaps out of his seat and presses something on my remote, causing the chair to disengage.

"You okay?" he asks, looming over me with concern on his face.

I put my sandals back on. "It was too intense. I

don't think I can carry on a conversation and use this chair at the same time."

He returns to his seat. "So... you are still willing to have a conversation?"

I roll my eyes. "Even if that means more of your silly get-to-know-each-other questions."

He pulls out his phone and glances at the screen. "In that case, if you could magically get rid of one bodily function, which one would you choose?"

"Seriously?"

He hides the phone. "Why would I not be serious?"

"Because bodily functions aren't usually part of polite conversation, outside of jokes. Unless a brain fart is a bodily function—because I think whoever created these questions must've had one." What I leave unsaid is that Lucius must've also had a brain fart when he chose to ask said questions.

He rubs his temples. "The correct answer is fine for polite conversation."

Is an eyeroll a bodily function? Because it happens again for me. "And what's the right answer? Sweating?"

"Sleep."

My eyebrows jump up—a bodily function you can fix with Botox instead of magic. "Is sleep even a bodily function?"

"An essential one," he says. "But since we're talking magical intervention, your health wouldn't suffer if you

149

gave it up in this scenario. Sleep is the one to get rid of because it takes up a whopping one-third of our lives."

Maybe a massage is exactly what I need to keep myself calm as I talk to him?

"Get-to-know-you questions are supposed to be open-ended," I say. "If they have right or wrong answers, that's a quiz."

"You ask something then," he says.

"Sure. Why would you want to get rid of a bodily function in the first place?"

He rubs his chin. "That's a good question. I guess it's my dislike of being biological."

I gape at him. "As opposed to what, metaphysical?"

He shakes his head. "One of the things I'm looking forward to in the future is uploading my brain's contents into a sturdier construct, and then living inside a body much better designed than this meat-sack." He looks down at himself disapprovingly.

Should I reassure him that the meatsack in question is actually very nice-looking? And that it's the brain inside it that could use some improvement—at least the parts responsible for social skills?

Nah.

Instead, I ask, "So... you wish you were a robot?"

"Or at least a cyborg," he says, deadpan.

"And you're sure you're not secretly a robot already?"

It would explain a lot.

He scoffs. "If I were a robot, sticks and stones wouldn't break my titanium bones."

I can't help but snort. "If we assume becoming a robot—or a cyborg—is a good idea, which it's not, isn't technology very far away from that?"

He shakes his head. "Many think so, but I believe it's just around the corner. Gram is already a cyborg—in that she has a cochlear implant. And if she ever developed severe retinitis pigmentosa, I could get her bionic eyes, which many people already have."

Wow. Bionic eyes already exist? I didn't realize. "I understand why you'd get a gizmo to restore function, but you're thinking of just ditching your body for shits and giggles." I grin at him. "And if you were a robot, you would not be able to do either of those things."

Did he just roll his eyes at me? "Don't tell me you're one of those who think the human body is perfect as is."

"I'd say *some* people's bodies are perfect." My treacherous non-bionic eyes can't help but scan his tall, hard-muscled frame.

"What about the throat?" he asks.

I look at his supremely masculine Adam's apple in confusion... and with a small dash of lust. "What about it?"

"Same passage for food and breathing," he says with disdain. "Do you know how many people choke? How many babies? And don't get me started on how easy the neck is to snap—and how irreparable the damage is that results from doing so."

Snap the neck? I hope he doesn't do it to me for asking, "Will your robot body have a blowhole, like in a dolphin?"

He's unfazed. "Assuming the body will require oxygen intake, maybe. Or maybe it will have solar panels, or use photosynthesis."

Ooh, I do like the latter idea. If I could perform photosynthesis, I'd be like a cactus.

I rub the back of my suddenly-less-useful-feeling neck. "That's just one body part. Why get rid of the rest?"

"That's just the start. Our knees are ridiculously easy to tear. Our taste buds crave things that are bad for our health. And, unlike most other animals, we do not produce essential nutrients, such as Vitamin C, in our bodies."

Huh. I never thought about it, but he's right. Deer eat only grass, but they never have a protein deficiency, nor do they take multivitamins. Still, a robot body seems like overkill.

Then it hits me. "This is just like the city you plan to build. You're trying to play God. To control *everything*."

He cocks his head. "You say that as if it were a bad thing."

I resist the urge to roll my eyes again. "I can't

believe I'm saying this, but I think I'm ready for the next question."

"If someone evil told you that you'll be forced to eat one type of food for a year, at every meal, which food would you choose?"

"That sounds horrible," I say and pause, thinking. "Maybe potatoes. I believe they have everything I need to survive. At least that was the case for Matt Damon in *The Martian*."

Lucius grins. "I was going to say bananas, but I like your answer better."

Our conversation continues in this vein for a while. We learn that he'd rather eat a superhot red pepper, whereas I'd choose a colonoscopy. If he were a car, he'd be a Tesla, while I'd be Citroën Cactus. And so on, including my favorite tidbit: when it comes to giving up personal hygiene to reach our goals, we both would do it.

Soon, it's brunch time, and it's a gourmet meal that turns out to have been prepared by one of Lucius's private chefs.

Yes, chefs, as in plural.

"If it didn't taste optimal, it's not the chef's fault," Lucius says after we're done. "Even with a humidifier, the air up here is cool and dry, which makes our taste-buds go numb. Another flaw of biology, in case you're keeping score."

I tilt my empty plate toward him. "If this is a less tasty version, your chef deserves a raise."

"I'll pass him your compliments," Lucius says. "Did you have any more get-to-know-you questions?"

I rub my protruding belly. "I might be too stuffed for that."

He sighs. "Another flaw of biological bodies—all the blood is used for digestion, leaving little for the brain."

I yawn. "When are we landing?"

He looks out the window. "At two p.m. Eastern time."

"What? Is it the lack of blood in my brain, or is that too quick?"

He grins. "This is a supersonic jet prototype. The flight is less than two hours. The change in time zones is the only reason we're landing in the afternoon."

Should I be surprised he's got the latest and greatest technological marvels at his disposal? The surprise is that he hasn't yet replaced Elijah with a self-driving limo.

"Would you mind if I got a massage?" he asks. "I like to do that if I can't walk after a meal."

I shake my head. "I could use one too."

We both activate our chairs, and I can't help but smile at the thought of this being a type of couple's massage.

Then the chair begins to work its magic, and combined with the scrumptious meal, I end up giving in to the pleasure of that bodily function Lucius resents so much—sleep.

It takes me a moment to gather my senses when I wake up.

Okay, I'm on the supersonic jet, and the massage chair is still running, which may explain why I feel like a custard.

Huh. Lucius is sleeping in his chair, but the plane isn't in motion anymore. How nice. On a regular plane, they wake you up when you land, but not here.

I clear my throat.

Lucius blinks open his eyes.

"I think we're here." I peek out the window at a green field. "Wherever 'here' is."

"A private airport," he says. "Come, the car is already waiting for us."

Surprise surprise, the car turns out to be a limo. I guess when you're as rich as Lucius, other types of cars refuse to give you a ride.

"What's the itinerary?" I ask as we get moving.

"Right now, I'm heading to the meeting I came here for," he says. "I'd appreciate it if you were to join me."

He would? "Why do you need me there?"

He shrugs. "The land owner called himself old-fashioned, so I figure he might feel more favorably toward a family man—or at least one attached to a beautiful woman."

If my heart were a cactus, it would bloom right

here and now at the "beautiful woman" description he's so casually tossed my way.

"Sure," I surprise myself by saying. "I'll join you."

Saguaro bite me. Why did I say that? I'm here to visit the UF campus, first and foremost.

Oh, well. I guess it's true what they say about the power of flattery.

————

The meeting takes place in a stately two-story building surrounded by impeccable landscaping. When we enter the conference room, I see why the landowner called himself old-fashioned. He's so ancient he probably predates the invention of fashion.

"This is Mr. Winston," Lucius says.

"I insist again," Mr. Winston says with a smile that deepens the grooves and creases around his eyes. "Call me John."

Lucius nods. "Sorry... John."

"Nice you meet you, *John*," I say. "My name is Juno."

"A pleasure, Juno." John looks at Lucius. "Are you kids married?"

"Dating," Lucius says.

"Ah," John says. "I used to do that in my day. I dated my wife for a whole week before we tied the knot."

A week? Things sure moved fast when you had to get married before hooking up.

"In any case." John takes a seat. "You make a beautiful couple."

"Thanks," Lucius and I say in unison and sit down too.

"How about we get down to business?" Lucius says, pulling out a folder with some papers.

They launch into a discussion about surveys and development that I mostly tune out, until a question by John perks up my ears.

"Will you take any steps to preserve local plant species?" he asks.

"Plant preservation," Lucius repeats with a frown. "I'm not—"

"Honey, would you mind if I jumped in?" I ask. I may not be business-savvy, but plants I know.

Lucius gestures with an open palm. "Please."

That may be the first please I've heard him utter, and the fact that he trusts me enough to speak at this important business meeting makes me feel things I shouldn't.

"I'm not sure if you realize this, but urban landscaping already uses about eighty different native species, which means they can easily be salvaged during development."

"Oh?" John's white caterpillar of a unibrow seesaws on his forehead.

Lucius nods, as if that has been the plan all along.

"Yes, thus saving on landscaping costs." He gives me an approving look.

Encouraged, I continue. "In fact, we could build an onsite nursery to store the salvaged plants. Whatever isn't used for Novus Rome could be sold to other developers."

"Fascinating," John says. "What are some examples of these plants?"

I take out my phone and do a search. "This here is red maple." I display the picture for them both.

"I recognize it," John says. "These would work well as shade plants."

I nod. "They would indeed, and birds and pollinators would thank us in the process." I show the next image. "This is American holly. It could provide privacy." I look up another one. "Highbush blueberry could make nice hedges."

Before I can search for something in the cactus family, John says, "Thank you so much. You've put my mind at ease." He turns his gaze to Lucius. "I'm ready to proceed with the deal."

Chapter 22

Lucius

As we sit across from each other in the limo, I study Juno.

Her assist at the meeting was amazing. I was caught off-guard by it, even though I shouldn't have been. She has a razor-sharp mind and an obvious love for plants. In my defense, even a trained botanist might not have been able to spout off facts about Florida's native flora so easily.

"Are you sure about going for that Botany degree?" I ask as the limo starts moving.

"Why?" She looks squinty all of a sudden. "You don't think I can finish it?"

Fuck. Have I put my foot in my mouth? "I view degrees as a means to an end," I say carefully. "Usually, the end is something to put on your resume. So what I meant was: are you sure you need to learn more about plants for the job of your dreams? Based on what you did at our meeting, you may be able to skip to the next step."

In a breath, her narrowed eyes widen to the size of quarters. "Was there a compliment in there?"

I resist the urge to grunt in frustration. "That wasn't clear?"

She bites her lip. "Not exactly, but thank you. To answer your question, I don't feel like I know everything there is to know about plants. I doubt I'll ever feel that way. Most of the jobs I want require a degree, so I wouldn't even get an interview without one. Besides"— her chin dips down—"I want to finish college just to prove I can."

"That's silly," I say, then see her frown. Clearly, my foot has dipped into my mouth again. Quickly, I add, "Obviously, you can."

The radiant expression on her face tugs at something deep inside me that I would rather remain buried. "You really think so?"

I nod.

She looks at the limo floor. "I'm not so sure."

"Why?"

She sighs. "Did the dossier you collected on me not mention my dyslexia?"

"No," I say. "But so what? Albert Einstein was dyslexic. So was Steve Jobs. And Henry Ford. Walt Disney as well. It's a long, industrious list, and they all got far in life long before text-to-speech technology." I grab her hand and give it a gentle squeeze. "I have no doubt someone as determined and clever as you will finish college *summa cum laude.*"

She beams at me. "I hope you're right."

"I know I'm right." Reluctantly, I let her hand go.

She looks at me with a strange expression—one that reminds me of the kiss I've been putting out of my mind. "Where are we going?"

"It's a surprise," I say.

Her breath catches, making me realize I'm staring at her chest. "A surprise?"

I force my eyes up. "A surprise is an event where you don't anticipate the outcome."

"Ah. So an example would be a whole minute where you're not an ass?"

I sigh. "We're going to The Florida Museum of Natural History."

Her eyes light up, like a jar of honey hit by a sunray. "Isn't that on the University of Florida campus?"

I can't resist a self-satisfied grin. "I figured you might like that."

"I'd love it! Can we stroll around the campus when we get there?"

"Of course." I think I'd stroll through sewers if it meant keeping that expression on her face.

Wait, what? If I were alone, I'd smack my meatsack

self... maybe in the dick—the likely culprit of these errant thoughts.

"Thanks." She licks her lips again, making it official.

Fucking biology is making me want to kiss her.

Again.

Chapter 23

Juno

LUCIUS STARES at me with an expression that's hard to puzzle out.

Is he regretting the nice gesture already? Or his earlier compliments? Or is that his constipated face?

"I need to check some work emails," he says, his tone gruff.

"Sure." Have I done something to offend him, or is he simply being his regular asshole self?

He pulls out his phone, so I take out my CD player and start my audiobook. At some point, I catch him looking at my device with derision.

Ah, that's right. Slightly dated technology annoys him.

I should've brought a steam engine.

"This is wonderful," I say as we enter the lush Butterfly Rainforest exhibit.

The brochure promised a thousand butterflies and moths of over fifty species, and the flying insects do not disappoint.

I've even forgotten that I'm slightly mad at Lucius for his abrupt one-eighty in the car.

"Yeah." He examines our colorful, serene surroundings. "This alone makes the trip to Gainesville worth it."

I reach out to touch his shoulder, then realize we're not in the kind of relationship that would make such a familiar gesture appropriate. "I'm sorry they don't have any stuff related to ancient Rome."

"I knew they wouldn't." He turns to me, eyes glinting devilishly. "No place is perfect."

His gaze captures me. I swallow thickly and take a step back before I do something crazy, like throw my lips at his. Even so, my voice is a bit husky as I say, "If I get accepted, I think I'll come here all the time."

"When," he says, turning to check out a particularly spectacular orchid. "Not if."

There are more butterflies in my belly than in this garden. He's doing that one-eighty again, only in the opposite direction—and I can't help lapping it up. First, he called me "determined and clever," and now he's certain I'll be accepted. Does he mean it? Then again, would he say it if he didn't? He's certainly not the type to lie in order to seem nice.

He glances at me in that moment, and our eyes catch again. My pulse picks up, the rhythm suddenly unsteady. I can see subtle flecks of blue in his steel-gray eyes, and my breath shallows out as unsettling warmth spreads through my body. I swallow hard as my gaze drops to his lips, the stern curve of which seems softer now that they're slightly parted.

Is he going to kiss me again? Am I going to let him?

I swallow again and sway toward him—only to jump as loud voices suddenly burst into my hearing range. Startled, I turn and see that a rambunctious group of young males has entered the exhibit.

Ugh. Not only have they interrupted what may have been another kiss, but they smell like a brewery and are wearing T-shirts with what seem to be the Greek letters *Alpha*, *Pi*, and *Epsilon*—next to a picture of an ape.

Speaking of apes, that's what they sound like—specifically, chimpanzees about to throw feces.

"Pledges," Lucius says, making it sound like a dirty word.

As if to confirm, one of them yells, "This is the Caterpillar Pledge!"

Yep. They're all holding handfuls of bugs, enough to make two more exhibits worth of moths and butterflies.

I stare in horror as the newcomers stuff their mouths with said caterpillars, like starved cuckoos. "Are they—"

I don't bother asking the rest of my question because as one, the dudes begin masticating.

Lucius grabs my hand. "Let's get out of here before the puking begins." He drags me behind him, pushing the caterpillar-munching idiots out of our way.

As we exit, suspicious gagging sounds begin—proving that Lucius was right.

"Still want to attend this fine educational establishment?" Lucius asks as we leave the museum premises.

I look around at the palm trees and the impeccably maintained green spaces. "Yep. I'll just skip the Greek life."

"That goes without saying," he says. "But fine. If you still want to attend, let's start the tour."

We do and it's nice—and not just because the UF campus is a dream. To my surprise, Lucius's company is what really cinches it for me, probably because he manages the miracle of saying nothing asshole-y throughout, just asks what classes I'll be taking once I get accepted (not sure), and if I plan to live on campus or not (even less sure).

When I tell him I'm getting tired of the tour, he mysteriously claims there's one more thing I just have to see and leads me somewhere.

Before I can get too curious, we turn a corner, and I spot a blanket spread out on a patch of grass, with a large basket sitting on it.

A picnic?

"I had Elijah arrange this small surprise," Lucius

says. "The food is courtesy of Gator Dining services—in case you're curious about what you'll be eating once you're accepted."

Wow. If I didn't know any better, I'd suspect him of trying to get into my pants.

"There isn't actual gator meat in there, right?" I ask as I sit on the blanket in lotus pose.

Lucius opens the basket and looks inside with a slight wrinkle of his nose. "Better not be."

I pull out a black plastic container and examine it. "Looks like chicken and pasta."

He opens his. "Smells edible."

He doesn't look too sure.

With an eyeroll, I dig in... and gag—in unison with Lucius.

"This chicken breast tastes like a shoe sole," I say after I manage to swallow the contents of my mouth. "I'm guessing Elijah asked for 'soul food' in his British accent, and they misunderstood."

Lucius spits his mouthful of pasta into the container. "Speaking of shoes, this pasta is chewier than laces. As flavorless too."

Has someone been spoiled by his personal chef? I take a dainty bite of the pasta—and barely manage to swallow it. Either I've also been spoiled, or this pasta is to the rest of its kind as Hitler was to the rest of humanity.

"Maybe those dumdums ate the caterpillars because they were an improvement on the cafeteria food?" I speculate.

Lucius takes out his phone and writes a quick text. Then he says, "This is embarrassing. Why don't I take you to our place? I just asked Elijah to make sure a *decent* meal is waiting for us there." In a sterner tone, he adds, "It will be made by my chefs, and Elijah will taste it, personally."

My eyebrow lifts of its own initiative. "*Our* place?"

He drops his plastic box into the basket. "I rented something here. Figured we wouldn't want to rush back to LA."

"As in... we're staying overnight?" Can he see my cheeks blushing?

He sighs. "In different rooms, obviously."

"Obviously." The pang of disappointment I feel is on par with my experience of this chicken and pasta, combined.

"If you want, I can arrange for you to fly back," Lucius says. "I just figured you'd want to see more of what Gainesville has to offer... Plus, we have a photoshoot tomorrow."

"A photoshoot?"

He explains how he wants to thwart the paparazzi by "leaking" flattering, professionally taken photos of the two of us, looking as happy as someone who doesn't eat UF cafeteria food.

"That sounds good," I say. "I'll stay."

We head to the limo. I'm not sure why, but despite his assurances of us sleeping in different rooms, I still feel like a virginal Victorian lady antici-pating a stroll with a rakish duke—without a chaperone.

———

"This is what you rented?" I say wonderingly as I stare at the sprawling mansion in front of us. The place looks too fancy, even for the luxury section of Airbnb.

Lucius merely shrugs. "This is the best I could do on short notice."

So, if he'd had time, he would've rented something like a magical castle? Maybe had someone build him a mansion from scratch?

"Should we check it out?" he asks.

I nod, and we spend a few minutes examining the property—which is as spacious inside as it looked from the outside.

When I notice the bored expression on Lucius's face, I can't help but say, "Too small?"

"It was supposed to be Colonial style," he says. "But it looks Mediterranean to me."

Seriously, I want his problems, just for a day.

Before I can respond, Elijah materializes, ninja-butler style. "Dinner is served."

———

The dinner is some delicious grain I don't recognize with lobster that's been garnished with caviar—because lobster without caviar is not ritzy enough.

It tastes so good I almost bite my tongue. "Seems like Elijah has overcompensated for the earlier blunder," I say, lowering my voice. "What grain is this?"

"Teff," Lucius says. "Shouldn't you know that? It was one of the earliest plants to be cultivated."

I resist the urge to hiss. "I don't know *everything* about plants. Just lots of things."

"It's also the smallest grain," he says professorially. "Originally grown in Ethiopia."

Instead of being annoyed, I make a mental note to read into edible plants so I don't look like a dummy ever again. Oh, and I'll get Lucius a book on manners. "Let's talk about something else."

Anything else.

"Like what?" he asks.

"Tell me about your grandmother." I eye another lobster piece hungrily. "After all, she is the catalyst for the fartlek."

Lucius smiles, revealing the full glory of his dimple. "Gram has many stories."

"Like what?"

"Well"—his smile widens—"she says she knew Andy Warhol."

"The one who painted *Campbell's Soup Cans*?"

Lucius nods. "Allegedly, they ate some Campbell's soup together."

"Wow."

"Yeah," he says. "And she loves music. Says she was caught up in Beatlemania, and before that, she was a huge Bob Dylan fan. Claims she even met him on *The Tonight Show, Starring Johnny Carson* in the summer of '63."

Huh. "Did she get to talk to him?"

"Perhaps more than just talk. Mom dropped unsolicited hints over the years that there might've been an affair there, but Gram never confirmed it. I never probed deeper because I'd rather not know about my grandmother's private life. Or my mother's." He says the last in a way that seems to imply his mom overshares—easy to believe in light of his earlier comment about Metallica.

"Your grandmother sounds fun," I say. His mom, not so much, but I don't point that out. "And you seem to know a lot about her."

"I do," he says. "I know that Gram's favorite book is *The Feminine Mystique* by Betty Friedan. Her favorite movie is *2001: A Space Odyssey*, and she was a huge fan of the moon race."

I cock my head. "Did you get your love of technology from her?"

He considers this for a second. "You know, it's possible."

"Does she also want to be a robot?"

"Not in so many words," he says. "Gram is skeptical that an artificially created body would allow all the

171

nuanced sensations and emotions that humans can feel. That's what it would take for her to put her brain into one."

"If that becomes possible, I'd consider shoving my brain into such a body," I say. "When I'm eighty, anyway."

Lucius points his lobster fork at me triumphantly. "So you're not as technophobic as I thought."

"Never said I was."

He clears his throat pointedly. "The CD player. The flip phone. You don't see how someone could get that idea?"

I roll my eyes. "When am I going to meet the legendary Gram?"

His phone dings.

He checks it and grins widely. "Jinx. She's just asked me when she's going to meet *you*."

"How about shortly after we're back?"

"You sure?" He glances at his phone, as though his grandmother can overhear us through it—and for all I know, maybe she can.

"Yeah. I'd love to meet her."

He fires off a text. "It's set up. No backing out now."

I eat another morsel, then ask, "Any last-minute things we should get to know about each other?"

"You haven't told me much about your family."

I purse my lips. "Did your dossier on me not go into that?"

He sighs. "Can you forget about that already?"

Can I? No. Can I pretend so we can continue the meal in relative peace? Sure. "Well, my parents and their parents are all nice people, with whom I have a great relationship. They all reside in or near Big Bear Lake, which is where I grew up."

He looks genuinely interested, or is a better actor than I thought. "What do they do?"

"My parents own a snowboarding company," I say. "Mom's parents own a fishery, and Dad's parents are retired teachers."

I pointedly don't go into detail about how disappointed my whole clan was when I moved to the big city, an entire two-hour drive away. Or about how I've so far foiled their dreams of lots of grandchildren and great-grandchildren. Or—

"Must be nice to have such a big family," Lucius says.

The hint of wistfulness in his tone makes something in my chest squeeze. "Is it just you, your mom, and your grandmother?"

"More my grandmother than my mom, but yeah."

"What about your dad and his family?"

His lips flatten. "My father wasn't there when I was growing up, so I have no interest in him now, and my grandparents on his side have passed away."

My hand reaches of its own accord to cover his. "One day, you're going to make a family of your own."

It will not be with me, but I'm sure the list of volunteers would stretch from here to Antarctica.

He glances at my hand with such a strange expression that I yank it back.

His face changes again.

Is that disappointment? Anger? Would his future face—the robotic one—also be this difficult to read?

After a few seconds of silence as uncomfortable as a bed of nails, he says, "I'm not sure I'm the type to make a family."

Chapter 24

Lucius

Fuck. Why did I say that?

Now there's pity in her eyes—and I loathe pity. What's worse is that I'm lying. I *can* picture a family pretty well—and she's in it, but that's crazy. The three-hour difference between California and Florida must've given me the worst case of jetlag in history—one that comes with delusions on top of everything else.

Or, more likely, I'm starting to forget the fartlek is not a real relationship.

I push my plate away, half the delicacies on it unfinished.

Juno regards me with confusion.

I stand up. "I've suddenly lost my appetite."

Now she gapes at me like lobsters are crawling out of my eyes and puking caviar.

Which makes sense. Even I, far from an expert on

manners, know that leaving her here mid-dinner is rude. But it's better than the alternative, which would be lashing out at a woman who's gone out of her way to be pleasant—even though that wasn't part of our contract.

Some inner decision made, she purses her lips and pushes her own plate away. "It's not your appetite. I think it's the time difference. It's not dinnertime back home."

I'm beginning to regret my impulsivity. Damn biology and the emotions that go along with it. Now we're committed to cutting dinner short and will both miss the lychee panna cotta that was going to be the dessert.

"Do you want me to show you your bedroom?" I ask, feeling like an idiot.

She shakes her head. "It's two corridors down, on the left, right?"

"Left, right," I say.

She doesn't say anything back, not even a thanks, so I fill the silence with, "There's a new toothbrush waiting there for you, and a tube of Sensodyne, as well as a bottle of Neutrogena shampoo and Dove body wash."

Fuck. Why did I blurt all that?

As expected, there's now a mutinous expression in her eyes. Before she can start with her signature snide remarks, I say, "I noticed the products you use when I peeked into your bathroom the other day. This isn't from the dossier."

She looks skeptical. However, all she says is, "Goodnight."

"Goodnight," I reply and stride into my bedroom, where I go through my evening routine before I realize how stupid that is.

We're three hours ahead, and it's not yet bedtime even in Florida.

Oh, well. I could use the alone time to work on Novus Rome—which now, thanks in part to Juno, has a plot of land.

————

At three a.m. local time—midnight at home—I strip to my boxers and head to bed.

An hour passes, but sleep doesn't come.

I debate jerking off, as is becoming a tradition.

Something stops me. Somehow, it feels wrong to do this with Juno so close. Or maybe I just feel pathetic settling for my fist when what I really want is—

No. I'm just hungry... for food. That's it. I bet if I eat some lychee panna cotta, I'll sleep like a drunk baby.

I slide my feet into slippers and march to the kitchen.

Huh.

Do I hear the sound of someone scurrying about in there? Also, what's with that light?

I carefully step inside. The light is coming from the refrigerator, and illuminated by it is Juno. She's wearing the sexiest, most sheer nightie I've ever seen and eating the panna cotta that was my goal straight out of the storage jar with her bare hands, like a starved animal.

I clear my throat. "Channeling a racoon?"

She nearly drops the precious jar, then examines me with a gasp, her gaze lingering on my naked torso. Then she licks her fingers clean, almost as an afterthought, and swallows everything with an audible gulp.

Fuck me. My biology is taking over my body completely. My nostrils flare and my legs carry me to the fridge—at the same time as my cock stirs, which means I should be anywhere but in Juno's company.

"What are you doing here?" she whispers when I'm close enough for another kiss.

As she talks, her chest heaves, making me aware of her pebbled nipples.

Am I dreaming this? I had a wet dream just like this the other night, only she wore even less.

With effort, I suppress my lurid imaginings and nod at the jar in her hands. "I have a craving... for panna cotta."

"Oh." She dips her index and middle fingers into

the jar again, only to then extend her hand toward me. "Want?"

Without a second of hesitation, I pounce. An eyeblink later, her fingers are in my mouth.

Juno's eyes widen. There's a real possibility she was joking about feeding me this way—or didn't think the offer through.

Well, it's too late now. I do to her fingers what I'm dying to do to her nipples... and pussy. I suck them gently, my tongue lapping every bit of deliciousness it encounters.

She drops the jar. With a dexterity I didn't know I possessed, I catch it mid-air and set it on the nearby counter—all without letting go of her now-panna-cotta-free fingers.

She jerks her hand away from my mouth, drops her gaze to take in my raging erection, and blushes like the strawberry that was meant to be the topping for the panna cotta.

When she meets my gaze again, her face is completely red and her voice is husky as she whispers, "You've got dessert all over your mouth."

I feel the truth of her statement with my tongue. Against my better judgement, a wicked grin stretches my mouth as I parrot her offer. "Want?"

Insanity is clearly contagious.

Her eyes flare, her chest heaves faster, and just when I think she's going to run away screaming, she grabs the back of my head and pulls my mouth to hers.

My heart rate surges. The last time, the kiss was amazing, but this time, it's maddening. My breathing turns ragged, my cock grows achingly hard, and all I want is to rip Juno's nightie off, like a caveman.

She moans into my mouth, her breath scented with the sweetness of the panna cotta as her tongue dances with mine.

Fuuuuck.

Where's that robot body when you need one? This biological one is out of control.

With a low growl, I grab her buttocks, lift her off her feet, and sit her on the counter, sweeping off the panna cotta and whatever else was there. Distantly, I hear the glass jar break as it hits the floor, and I pull away from the kiss, breathing hard.

She looks out of breath also, her face even more flushed. Glancing down, I see her legs spread in front of me like an offering. My heartbeat speeds up further. She's wearing panties, but like the nightie, they are sheer.

The urge to rip fabric into shreds intensifies.

"I have a new idea for dessert," I say hoarsely without taking my eyes off the prize.

She licks her lips. Her eyes are heavy-lidded as she nods. Taking that for permission, I grip the flimsy fabric of her panties and pull it aside, none-too-gently. It rips in my grasp. Oh, well. I guess that was meant to be.

Mouth watering, I bend over the dark patch of

curls exposed to my gaze. I love that she's all natural, like the perfect Roman goddess that she is. Reverently, I kiss her thigh. Her skin is soft and silky to the touch, and she gasps as I place another kiss higher up.

The spot I kissed pebbles with goosebumps.

I shift to move my lips higher yet—only to jolt at a strange sound by the kitchen entrance.

Then a thousand ceiling sconces light up, blinding me with sudden brightness.

What the hell?

I jerk to my feet and glare at the source of the distraction—Elijah, who's pointing a fucking revolver at me, of all things.

An ancient-looking revolver at that—trust Elijah and his butlery sensibilities to get an antique.

At the sight of Juno and me, his eyes go wide and his face red. "I'm so sorry, sir!" He lowers the gun. "I thought you were an intruder and—"

I'm not listening. Grabbing a stunned Juno, I set her on her feet behind me, onto one of the few areas of the floor clear of the mess I've made.

Making sure her body is hidden from view by mine, I round on Elijah, not bothering to hide my wrath. "A fucking gun?"

My butler looks like he wants to sink through the floor. "This *is* Florida, sir."

"Sure, I must have missed it when they were handing out deadly weapons as we exited the plane. Antiques, at that."

"I'm terribly sorry, sir." Elijah backs away. "I'll get the lights on the way out."

Except Elijah is not looking where he's going and his foot lands on a large shard of glass resting in a splatter of panna cotta. Predictably, the shard slides— like a banana peel in a fucking cartoon. As if acting out a scene from that same cartoon, Elijah flails his arms wildly before falling on his ass.

The gun slips from his grasp, hitting the floor with a clank of metal on tile.

Before I can move to help, a deafening boom assaults my eardrums—followed by an explosion of pain.

Chapter 25

Juno

EVERYTHING THAT HAPPENED after Lucius walked in on me in the kitchen was dream-like. His licking my fingers, the kissing... of lips and elsewhere. When Elijah barged in with a gun, it was just as surreal as the rest—that is, until the gun went off.

As soon as the *bang* hits my ears, an overdose of adrenaline smashes sanity into my brain. Lucius staggers, grabbing his head, and to my horror, I see that it's gushing blood as if it were its job.

Gasping, I rush toward him, as does Elijah, who's managed to scramble to his feet despite sliding in the panna cotta a few times.

"Sir!" His British accent is extra thick. "I shot you!"

That was my initial fear as well, but with the clarity only possible when one is on the verge of a heart attack, I spot bits of broken glass around Lucius.

I dart a glance at the ceiling.

A sconce is missing.

"I think you shot the light fixture," I yell at Elijah. "That's what fell on him!"

I kneel next to Lucius, who's now sitting on the floor and muttering a stream of curses. Graphic, eloquent curses. I take the richness of his vocabulary as a good sign. If he had brain damage, he'd be drooling or something like that.

Amazed that I'm not a whimpering mess, I coo soothingly to Lucius as I gently move his hand away to assess the situation. The bleeding is insane, but there's no sign of glass sticking out of his head, nor a bullet wound for that matter. Nor do I see any bone or leaking brains.

Elijah is wringing his hands and doing circles around us. "I'm so, so sorry, sir!" He sounds on the verge of crying.

I peer up at him with a frown. "You okay?"

He nearly trips again as he tries to look at Lucius's bleeding head. "I shot him! Oh, dear Lord, I shot him."

My frown transforms into a glare. "I mean, is your coccyx bone okay? You *did* fall on your butt."

Elijah waves that away. "I knew eating all those biscuits would come in handy one day."

"Get me alcohol," I order. "And prepare to take us to the hospital. Quickly."

Looking grateful to have something to do, Elijah rushes away.

"The hospital?" Lucius presses his hand to the wound again, then looks down at the blood covering his palm. His face turns pale. "How bad is it?"

Pretty bad, at least in my non-medical opinion. "You're fine," I say soothingly. "Just a precaution."

He seems to relax at that, so I jump up and run toward the fridge, intent on finding some ice.

"Stop!" Lucius's voice strengthens. "You're going to step on broken glass."

He's got a point. There are jar pieces everywhere, and I was dumb enough to come down here barefoot.

"I'll be careful," I say, cautiously stepping over a couple of shards before reaching the freezer.

I open it.

The thing is almost empty. The only item inside is a bag of frozen pizza bagels.

I pull those out, just in time to spot Elijah coming back into the room with a bottle of rubbing alcohol and an industrial-sized box of gauze pads.

"An ambulance is on the way," Elijah says, panting. "Or we can take the limo, which will be ready in two minutes."

"Bring her shoes before she cuts her feet," Lucius barks at his poor butler. Then, examining my body with narrowed eyes, he adds, "Also bring her something more substantial to wear."

How can he be so bossy with an injury like that? Also, who cares what I wear?

Elijah turns to obey the order, but I call out, "Wait!

Leave the alcohol. Also, what's with this?" I wave the pizza bagels and nod at the empty freezer.

"The master eats those on occasion." Elijah sets the medical supplies on the counter. "They remind him of childhood."

"Fine. Go. And please get him some clothes too."

Elijah runs off, and Lucius reminds me to mind the glass as I move around.

Walking carefully, I grab the medical supplies and bring them over to where Lucius is sitting.

"This will sting," I say as I open the alcohol.

He takes a breath and nods.

I dump a few ounces onto the still-gushing wound. Lucius tenses but maintains a stoic silence as I arrange half the gauze pads in the box around the wound, then press them down with the pizza bagels.

"I figure the cold should prevent swelling," I say, mostly to myself. "And maybe help with coagulation."

"I think I'm fine," Lucius says. "It was just the shock of it."

The bleeding has stopped, but I don't dare let go of the pizza bagels.

"Let me check your pupils." I peer into his eyes.

Hmm. Are the pupils supposed to be dilated or constricted in a concussion situation? In any case, his seem normal, but what do I know? "Are you nauseated?" I ask, since that one is more obvious.

If he is, it's bad.

He shakes his head and winces.

"Use words," I say sternly. "Among other things, I need to hear if you're slurring." That also wouldn't be good, I'm pretty sure.

"I'm not nauseated. I also don't have ringing in my ears," he states. "And I haven't lost my sense of smell or taste."

I frown. "Are those also signs of a concussion?"

"I think so," he says, but he doesn't sound too sure.

"This is exactly why we need a doctor."

Elijah runs into the room, carrying a stock of clothes and shoes.

"Careful," I tell him. "If you slip again, who's going to help me carry Lucius to the limo?"

Lucius scoffs. "I'm not going to be carried."

"You are."

He shakes his head and grimaces again. "Once you're dressed, Elijah will help me stand."

I grab what Elijah brought for me, which is a pair of heels and an oversized hoodie that I packed for the plane ride, in case it got chilly at thirty thousand feet. Or however high supersonic jets go. Needless to say, the hoodie does *not* go with the heels, but I'm not about to chide the butler, who still seems to be on the verge of crying. He must also be in some kind of shock, given his choices for Lucius—a suit jacket, sweatpants, and hiking boots. No socks.

Okey-dokey. Lucius pulls on the sweatpants and

the boots as I hold the pizza bagels to his head. Then I instruct him to hold the bagels, and I turn to Elijah, who's now just standing there like a statue.

"Help me get him up," I order, and the butler springs into action, looking pathetically grateful to have me take charge.

Lucius exercises his colorful vocabulary once more as Elijah and I help him to his feet.

"Any vertigo?" I ask when he's fully vertical.

He starts to shake his head, then remembers to use his words in time. "I'm fine. I don't need a doctor."

I point at the puddle of blood on the floor where he was sitting, and he goes pale again, shutting up as I drape one of his arms over my shoulders and Elijah does the same on the other side. Together, the three of us make it out of the mansion and onto the driveway, where the limo already awaits.

"You don't think we should wait for the ambulance?" Elijah asks, sounding a bit more like himself.

"No," Lucius says imperiously. Now that we're away from all the blood, he seems more like his bossy self as well.

"I agree," I say. "We'll get there faster this way."

We get Lucius into the limo, where I order him to lie down on the seat and let me hold the defrosting bagels.

"I'll make all the arrangements as we drive," Elijah says.

I nod, and he closes the door as I perch next to

Lucius's head. The limo pulls out, and I overhear Elijah speaking sternly on the phone before the partition goes up.

Some of my adrenaline leaks out. Overcome with a sudden wave of emotion, I stroke Lucius's arm with my free hand. "How much does it hurt?" I ask softly.

"I'll be fine," he says, closing his eyes.

"You'd better be." A surge of belated terror hits me. "That bullet could've struck *you* instead of the sconce."

He opens his eyes, his face turning grim as he growls, "It could have hit *you*. I'll make Elijah rue the day he—"

"Don't. The poor man is already kicking himself."

Lucius's nostrils flare. "As he should. At the very least, he'll never touch a gun again."

That's probably a good idea. Lucius has enough money to hire professional bodyguards if he so chooses. There's no need for an armed butler.

"Do you know where the hospital we're going to is?" I ask.

"No. Can't be far, though, or I imagine we'd take the helicopter."

"What helicopter?"

He shifts his position. "The one I rented for the stay."

I change which hand is holding the bagels before I get frostbite. "A helicopter? That sounds like a reasonable expense."

Lucius smiles faintly. "It's to survey the land I came here to acquire."

Would he be this good at coming up with retorts if he had a concussion? Knowing him, probably.

I warm my free hand as best as I can with my breath, then lightly massage his shoulder. The hard muscle immediately relaxes under my touch, and the creases on his forehead smooth out, encouraging me to keep going.

Lucius closes his eyes, making me think he's drifting off, but then he opens them. "Look, Juno..." His voice is gruff. "About what happened before Elijah interrupted. I—"

"Don't," I say, a touch too sharply. If he were to say that was another round of PDA practice, I'd punch him, and then I'd feel super guilty doing that to someone in his condition. "We don't need to talk about it."

The creases in his forehead return, and I can tell he wants to push the issue. To my relief, he doesn't. He just closes his eyes again, and this time, I stroke his chest, trying not to think about how glad I am that there's no bullet hole in the warm, hard-muscled flesh.

The limo comes to a stop.

The doors open, and Elijah helps me get Lucius out.

When I turn around, I see that we're near the front doors of a hospital. A man and a woman are waiting for us there. He's dressed in a suit, and she's in scrubs.

They introduce themselves, and it turns out that he is the hospital president and she—and I quote—is "the best neurosurgeon in the state of Florida."

"Call me Dr. Brainiac," she says with a grin. "That's what my friends calls me, so why not people who wake me in the middle of the night, right?"

Wasn't Brainiac a villain in the Superman comics?

"Have a seat," Dr. Brainiac says, and only then do I notice the wheelchair.

"No," Lucius says sharply. "I can walk on my own."

Dr. Brainiac looks up at him skeptically. "You don't sound like someone with a bullet in his brain."

Lucius glares at her. "I didn't get shot."

Elijah studies his feet. "I might not have been entirely truthful. The bullet hit a ceiling sconce, and that's what fell on his head. Or a shard of it, at any rate."

Dr. Brainiac narrows her eyes. "And that's what entered his brain?"

"I doubt it," I chime in. "There's a gash there, but it doesn't look that deep."

She eyes me like I'm the only reasonable person here. "So why am I here?"

I nod at Elijah. "He made the arrangements."

"It's his head," Elijah says, sounding defensive. "Had it been his chest, I would've gotten the best cardi-ologist."

"By that logic, you need to see a proctologist about your fall," Lucius deadpans.

Elijah rubs his behind with a thoughtful expression.

"Fine. Whatever," Dr. Brainiac says. "We're here. Go ahead and take a seat."

Lucius looks at the wheelchair the way I would at a camel eating a cactus. "Like I said, my legs work just fine."

"Men and their egos," Dr. Brainiac mutters under her breath. She gestures at the president. "It's his hospital policy."

The president looks resolute. "Even if you had a papercut emergency, you'd enter in that chair."

With an exasperated sigh, Lucius sits his butt down, like a Roman emperor on his throne.

"Can I push?" Elijah asks.

"Sure," Lucius says. "Just you watch where you're going this time."

Mean, but not unreasonably so, all things considered.

When we reach the elevator, the president leaves us in the hands of Dr. Brainiac, and she takes us to a room that looks more like a five-star hotel suite than a hospital room. The only clue to this being a medical establishment is all the scary equipment.

Must be some sort of VIP room. Between this, the neurosurgeon, and the president, I wonder if Elijah committed Lucius to buying this hospital a new wing.

"You can have a seat there," the doctor says to Lucius and points at the comfiest-looking patient chair ever. "You two can take the couch," she tells me and Elijah. Then she grins again as she notices the bagels. "Some patients bring comfort blankets, but I say comfort food is more practical."

Lucius doesn't look amused in the slightest as he hands the semi-defrosted bag to the doc, who tosses it onto a nearby table. She then puts on gloves, removes the gauze pads, and peers at the wound. "Like snitches, you'll need some stitches."

Saguaro help us. Dr. Brainiac clearly wants to switch her career from neurosurgeon to comedian. Lucius does *not* look entertained.

Ignoring his glower, she walks over to the table and picks up a pair of tweezers and a tube of cream.

"This is a topical anesthetic," she says. "You want me to use it?"

"No," Lucius says grimly.

"I had a feeling you'd say that. Suit yourself. This will not hurt me one bit."

With that, she sticks the tweezers into the wound.

I feel a strong urge to cut a bitch, but Lucius bears the pain stoically, so I calm myself down.

Looking triumphant, Dr. Brainiac pulls out a tiny shard of glass and shows it to everyone. "If only all surgery were this easy."

Damn. That was there all this time?

She then grabs some iodine and applies it liberally

around the wound, at which point I stop looking because seeing the stitching might just cause me to get violent... or faint.

"That's it," Dr. Brainiac says after all of a minute. "Now drink this."

When I look back, Lucius's head is covered in bandages, making him look like a mummy, and he's sipping apple juice from a kiddie box.

Elijah stands up. "What do you mean? What if he's got a concussion?"

"Given how little swelling there is around the cut, the impact wasn't bad. Nor is he showing a single symptom of a concussion. The sugar in the juice should help him recover after the little bit of blood loss."

"But shouldn't you run some tests?" Elijah demands.

She shrugs. "In my professional opinion, this is a case of an ouchie boo-boo. My prescription would be to eat those bagels in the morning. But if you want to waste your time on tests, I can order some."

Lucius rises to his feet, looking much steadier than before. The juice has clearly worked its magic. "If the neurosurgeon thinks I'm fine, I'm fucking fine."

Dr. Brainiac flashes him her signature grin. "Make that a neurosurgeon who doesn't want her malpractice insurance to go up. Or one who doesn't wish to read the following article in the gossip columns: *Doctor's negligence kills billionaire.*"

"In that case, thank you very much, doctor," Elijah says stiffly.

"You're welcome," she says. "If you ever do get your brain damaged, or have a tumor you need removed, give me a call."

Elijah pales. "Let's hope it doesn't come to that. Once again, apologies for waking you up in the middle of the night."

She shrugs again. "My bank account would say, 'It's been a pleasure.'"

Without further ado, Lucius strides out of the room, and we hurry after him.

Once inside the limo, Lucius yawns and closes his eyes.

What a great idea. I close mine too—and must drift off, because a second later Elijah is rousing me.

"You okay?" I ask Lucius when we enter the mansion and Elijah scurries away to deal with the kitchen mess.

"Yeah," he replies wearily as we stop in front of the staircase leading up to the bedrooms. "Just need some sleep."

What I feel like saying is, "And I want to watch you sleep," but instead I go with the much less creepy, "Me too."

He kisses me gently on the cheek. "Thanks for fussing over me on the way to the hospital. It really helped."

With that bombshell, he goes up the stairs, leaving

me standing there with my palm pressed against my cheek and my mind spinning with all sorts of questions.

Chapter 26

Lucius

When I wake up, the top of my head is a little sore, but that's about it. I can't believe I was made to go the hospital with something so trivial. I think I allowed that to happen because I was in shock—not from Elijah's clumsy assassination attempt but from what happened between me and Juno.

As soon as I recall that encounter in the kitchen, I get hard. Does this mean I have regenerated all the blood I lost? Probably. I know this much: instead of me taming my biology, Juno is turning me into my biology's slave.

With a sigh, I take off the bandages and use a second mirror to examine the wound. It doesn't look bad, and my hair should cover it all nicely. Still, just in case, I'd better steer clear of Gram until full recovery.

When I'm done with my morning routine, I check my phone to remind myself of today's plans.

Ah, right. The photoshoot. That's an activity Juno and I can do that seems relatively safe... as far as biological urges are concerned.

———

Boy, was I wrong.

Juno looks extra sexy for the shoot—which, in hindsight, makes sense. She's female and we're about to take pictures.

Oh, well.

I do my best to smile instead of gritting my teeth when the photographer asks me to embrace her. As I do, her earthy, wonderful scent makes me as light-headed as when I lost all that blood last night.

"Smile," the photographer says.

With an effort, I lift the corners of my lips.

"A real smile," he says.

Should I tell him that it's hard to smile when you're trying not to get hard?

"Say cheese," he urges.

Could Juno's body heat melt cheese? The thought makes me smile, which brings the photoshoot to a blissful conclusion.

"So, what now?" Juno asks me after we get into the limo.

Great question. Whatever it is, it'll be best if we're not alone, or else what happened last night could happen again—and that would be a mistake for many reasons, but especially because she made it clear she regrets it. How else can I interpret her refusal to even talk about it?

To that end, we check out two amazing parks: Ichetucknee Spring and Devil's Millhopper—the latter being the only attraction I've heard of that's located in a gigantic sinkhole.

With every minute, I feel more comfortable in Juno's presence. I would even go as far as to say I genuinely enjoy her company. Which is a problem, one to which I think I have a solution. So, as we return to the limo, I ask, "When do you need to go back home?"

She sighs. "Soon, I'm afraid. I have to take care of all of my clients' plants. They can only wait so long to get watered."

"That settles it," I say. "We'll take you to the plane."

Her eyebrow arches. "Me? What about you?"

"I've decided to stay behind for a few days. I still need to survey the land, sign all the papers, and hopefully get the ball rolling on getting all the permits."

I'm not great at reading people, but I think Juno looks disappointed—though it's probably because all our nature hikes have come to an end, not because she will miss my company.

"What about the visit to your grandmother?" she asks. "I thought that was soon."

"It'll be the first thing we do when I get back," I say. "I'll set it all up, don't worry."

"Okay." She chews on one deliciously plump lip. "But... could we talk on the phone before that?"

I cock my head, puzzled. "Why?"

She shifts from foot to foot. "So we can learn more about each other. Your grandmother is the main reason for the fartlek, after all."

That makes sense to me. I nod decisively. "Sure. I'll call you."

And why not? It should be safe.

It's not like I can almost-eat her pussy over the phone.

Chapter 27

Juno

I FEEL melancholy on the flight back to LA.

I clearly liked Gainesville more than I thought I would. I miss it already. And it goes without saying, but I'll say it anyway: it is *not* my fake boyfriend that I'm moping about. Nope. It's the city of Gainesville, and I'm sticking to that.

When I get home, I finally call Pearl back—she's been trying to get an update on my "relationship," so I have to very pointedly remind her that a) a lady doesn't kiss and tell, and b) I've signed an NDA.

After Pearl lets me go, I prepare jugs of water with fertilizer in them. These are common tools of my trade, and I'll need them to revitalize the pothos plants at the Smiths' Family Estate—one of my key clients.

As I listen to my audiobook and take care of the plants, I almost manage to forget about what happened in Florida—the hot encounter in the kitchen, the terror of Lucius getting hurt, and how date-like all the hiking in the parks felt.

Fine, *almost* might not be the right word, but at least I don't dwell on all those things every waking moment.

Only most of them.

I'm just about done with the Smiths when my phone rings.

My heart leaps.

Is it Lucius already?

Nope. It's my mom.

"Hi, sweetie," she says.

"Hi," I say, doing my best not to sound disappointed. "How are things?"

"You're on speaker phone," my dad chimes in.

Hmm. This is rare. I wonder why—

"Why didn't you tell us you're dating?" Mom demands.

"And someone famous at that," Dad adds.

And there it is.

"Your grandmother saw you in a picture in a magazine," Dad says.

"You looked so pretty in it," Mom adds. "But you should have told us."

How does "pretty" logically flow into "told us?" I

cover the microphone so they don't hear me sigh, then explain about the NDA.

"But how serious is it?" Mom presses.

"The NDA forbids me from saying," I reply.

"Does he treat you well?" Dad demands.

"I wouldn't be with someone who doesn't," I say. "And there, you've just made me break the NDA."

The conversation—or rather, interrogation—continues in that vein for a while longer.

"How about you bring him over?" Mom finally suggests.

I nearly drop the phone. "Bring him?"

That's the craziest idea I've ever heard. If Lucius were a real boyfriend, I'd wait a year so as not to spook him.

"What a wonderful idea," Dad says. "That way, we can see what's what for ourselves, and you won't break the NDA."

Sure. That's assuming Lucius would agree to this madness, and there's no way he would.

"Please, honey," Mom says. "If not for me, do it for your grandparents."

Great. Guilt trip masquerading as an argument. "I can ask him," I say reluctantly.

"Promise?" Mom says.

"Yes."

"Great. Let me know when. Bye."

She hangs up before I can change my mind. So evil. Also, it's just occurred to me that Mom implied my grandparents would be at this hypothetical get-together. That's the sort of thing I'd put my boyfriends through only after we were engaged.

Oh, well. I don't need to worry, as all this is moot. Lucius will obviously say no, and then my conscience will be clear. Or clearer, which is the best I can hope for considering all the lies.

———

"I don't think he'll call today," I tell El Duderino after I finish my dinner and check his soil.

Dude. If you want to talk to this dude, why not call him yourself?

Hmm. Maybe I should. He's injured, so I might not look so desperate if I inquire about his health.

It would even be the polite thing to do.

Dude. You're overthinking this. Just call. The dude will be happy to—

My phone rings. I check the screen, then look at my cactus triumphantly. "It's Lucius."

Dude. You speak of this dude, and he calls. Just like that Devil dude.

I take a deep breath, trying to tamp down on my excitement as I pick up and say hi.

"Hello," Lucius says.

No "how are you?"

I'm just going to assume that was implied, so I say,

"I'm doing great. Got a chance to catch up on work. How about you?"

"My day was productive. The land is finally mine, and it's perfect for Novus Rome."

I squeeze the phone tighter. "I meant 'how does your head feel?'"

"Then why didn't you say *that*?" he asks.

"Touché. *How does your head feel?*"

"Much better. The worst thing about that whole mess is the endless stream of apologies from Elijah. I'm not sure if he's going for irony, but I've got more of a headache thanks to *that* than from his gunslinging."

"You poor baby, you've got a loyal employee who feels bad after he caused you bodily harm." I look at my cactus with exasperation.

Dude. Easy on the sarcasm. The dude was mortally injured.

"Touché," Lucius says. "But that's enough about that."

I walk over to my bed and sit on the edge. "Fine. There was something I wanted to ask you, actually. Or more like, I promised my parents to ask you, but I'm sure you'll say no, and that's fine."

"Promised to ask me what?"

I bite my lip. "They've learned about us thanks to some magazine article and—"

"Did the magazine use the photos from our shoot?" he asks.

"I didn't ask that," I say. "Because that wasn't the point."

"What was?"

I sigh. "That they think I have a boyfriend."

"That's implied."

"And so..." I take a breath. "They'd like to meet you. But I totally understand if—"

"Yes," he says confidently.

"Yes?" I stare at El Duderino in confusion.

Dude. I totally didn't expect this dude to agree to that either.

"Did you want me to say no?" Lucius asks, and I can picture him smirking on the other end of the call.

Yes. No. Maybe. "Why would I ask you if I didn't want you to go?"

I fully expect him to say, "Because you promised your nosy parents." Instead, he says, "It's a good idea."

Once again, I gape at my cactus.

Dude. I have no idea why this dude thinks it's a good idea.

"Why?" I finally ask.

"Great practice," Lucius says. "If your family buys the fartlek, so will Gram."

Of course. Makes sense. So why do I feel so disappointed by his robot-like logic?

"It's settled then," I say. "We'll do it when you're back."

If anyone learns about me meeting his grandmother and him meeting all my folks, they'll assume we're on the fast track to a shotgun wedding.

"Is there anything I should prep ahead of time?" he asks.

"Like what?" It would probably be prudent to have everyone in my family sign NDAs, but I'm not going to give him *that* idea.

"Are there any get-to-know-you questions we haven't covered that they might raise?"

I sigh. "They'll probably tell you the most embarrassing things about me, so out of fairness, maybe you could tell me yours?"

His sigh sounds a lot like mine. "Gram will probably tell you my most embarrassing stories also."

"Like?"

He tsk-tsks. "I'll only tell you mine if you tell me yours."

I hesitate, but then I figure why the hell not. He already knows I'm dyslexic. Softly, I say, "I doubt my family will tell you this, but my most embarrassing moments all have to do with my reading woes. I had a sadistic teacher who always called on me to read out loud. Some examples of my mishaps include 'vaginal ice cream' instead of 'vanilla' and 'period red' instead of 'Persian red.' Everyone had fun at my expense, and kids being kids, they mocked me for months afterward."

"Kids can be animals," he says with feeling. "And it

sounds like that teacher should've been fired... at the very least. What's her name?"

"Oh, don't worry, I got even." I smile at the memory. "I snuck Krazy Glue onto her seat. It ended with a pretty embarrassing trip to the hospital for her."

"Good." There is a smile in his voice as he says, "I'd better not piss you off."

"That's right. And to that end, you now owe me something embarrassing—and not what your grandmother will tell me."

Did he just curse under his breath?

"Fine," he says with obvious reluctance. "But this is doubly covered by our NDA."

"Sure." I mentally rub my hands together. He's obviously going to tell me something juicy.

"There was this bully who pantsed me in the cafeteria one time," he says.

I grit my teeth. "He what?"

"Pulled my pants down," Lucius clarifies.

I knew that, but I don't interrupt again.

"Anyway," Lucius continues. "I was wearing my Spartacus-themed underwear—and kids being kids, everyone laughed. But that wasn't the end, or the worst of it. Somehow, Gram learned about what happened, and she showed up the next day at the school. I have no idea how she knew which kid was the culprit, but she shouted at him in front of everyone, then pulled down *his* pants before she left."

I gasp.

"Yeah," Lucius says dryly. "It's lucky there were no security guards or teachers as witnesses, or else she'd be on some list. In any case, everyone called me 'granny's boy' for the rest of middle school."

Is it weird that I don't disapprove too much of his Gram's behavior? Her main mistake was that she did the deed publicly, thus embarrassing Lucius. She should've found the bully alone and then—

No. Wait. What am I thinking? She pulled down a child's pants. That's wrong to do anywhere, but infinitely more so in private.

"You win," I say. "If I had ended up with my pants down in my middle school cafeteria, I would've needed therapy for years."

"I didn't realize this was a contest."

I chuckle. "Can't you just accept your win gracefully?"

"I insist that you're the winner of this contest anyway, but I can't say why as I promised not to mention the event in question."

I flush. Of course! How could I have forgotten? The most embarrassing moment of my life was peeing in that elevator, hands down.

"I'm sorry," Lucius says, sounding genuinely contrite. "I shouldn't have mentioned *that which isn't to be spoken about*."

"Yeah. That was a low blow, especially to make a point."

He sighs. "I feel like I owe you another embarrassing story now."

"At least."

"Okay, here goes," he says. "This was in high school. I was walking with my lunch and sneezed at the wrong time. My pasta ended up all over me. Of course, the girl I liked saw the whole thing and laughed."

"That bitch." Oops, that might've been an overreaction.

"Hey, in her defense, it *was* funny."

I chew on the inside of my cheek, feeling irrationally upset. "Did you ask her out anyway?"

"No," he says, a little too sharply. "In any case, now that we're even, I'd better go."

Okay. A bit too abrupt, but fine. "Goodnight."

He hangs up.

Was it something I said?

Either way, the end of the conversation notwithstanding, that was kind of nice.

I hope he calls me tomorrow.

———

He does call, and our conversation goes much smoother this time. We talk more about our days in school, and he shares some stories about college. I also learn about his second passion after Ancient Rome: futurism. He and his fellow futurists love to ponder what new technological advancements are on the horizon, and how they will change life as we know it.

As we're saying goodbye, he promises to call again tomorrow.

Once again, he keeps his promise, and the highlight of this conversation is my question about his first kiss. As usual, he forces me to go first, and I admit that mine was in kindergarten, with a boy I played marriage with. The kiss was the "consummation" of that union. After teasing me about being a married woman, Lucius admits that his first kiss happened after he made his first million in his early twenties—in other words, crazy late. When I probe as to why he took so long to get to that milestone, he gets uncomfortable, so I drop the topic lest he doesn't call again.

The next day, our chat is downright pleasant, in part because I tell him interesting facts about cactuses, like how slowly the saguaro cactus grows, at a rate of only one and a half inches every ten years—yet, mind-bogglingly, the majestic plant grows to eighty feet tall. On his end, Lucius tells me so much about Ancient Rome that I feel like I've taken a trip there via a time machine.

And so it goes. Each day, our conversations get longer and longer, until they start to remind me of the way it was with my first boyfriend back in high school. Just like then, I often find myself with my phone in bed, talking until midnight, which is late into the night for Lucius on the East Coast.

We learn so much about each other that we could convince the CIA we're really dating. Our families don't stand a chance.

It's great, but there's one problem.

As the days go by, I begin to miss him. The calls, informative as they are, are no substitute for his magnetic presence.

It's dumb, but I can't help it.

Some part of me has clearly forgotten how fake our arrangement is.

Chapter 28

Lucius

"How is that cat doing?" I ask Juno as my limo drives to the private airport where my plane is parked. We've been chatting all through my packing, and I'm still not ready to get off the phone.

She laughs—a sound I find strikingly pleasant, especially as of late. "Are you really inquiring about the fluffy would-be-murderer? Clearly, we've run out of things to talk about."

I yawn, glancing out the window at the darkness outside. "You've got a point."

"Stop yawning," she says, then yawns loudly. "The cat is doing great, but her mom is going to murder me, thanks to the NDA you made me sign. If gossip were a person, it would be Pearl."

I frown. For some reason, I get annoyed whenever I'm reminded of the NDA, or other details that highlight the true nature of our arrangement.

"Speaking of the NDA," Juno says. "You have to tell me what I can and can't speak about when we visit my parents tomorrow."

My limo stops, and I exit it as Elijah gets the bags. "If in doubt, you can look at me," I say. "I'll blink if it's okay to share whatever you've started to talk about."

"If you blink too much, they'll think you've got conjunctivitis."

I ascend the stairs to the plane and take my seat. "How about you sit next to me at your parents' table," I say to Juno as I activate the massage feature. "If I want you to stop speaking, I'll step on your foot."

"Gently," she warns.

I grin. "I'll make it feather light."

"Okay."

"Good. Now I have to hang up. We're taking off in a minute."

"I can't believe I'll finally see you tomorrow," she says, and something in her voice makes my chest go tight yet light at the same time.

I also feel a pang of guilt. There's a tiny chance I stayed longer in Florida because I was dreading what might happen when I see her again.

What biology might make me do.

"Anyway, go," she says, but I don't hear the line disconnecting.

"Well, hang up," I say, reluctant to do so myself.

"No, you hang up."

Seriously? "No, ladies first."

"Age before beauty," she says.

I don't know what's more ridiculous, this back-and-forth or my strange stubbornness.

The plane's engines come to life with a roar.

"You hear that?" I ask. "It's going to be too noisy to talk in a second."

"So... hang up," she says.

I almost insist that she do it first, but I decide to be the grownup. "See you tomorrow," I say and reluctantly end the call.

———

The next day, as Elijah drives me through the gorgeous snowy peaks surrounding the calm waters of Big Bear Lake, I try to imagine what it was like for Juno to grow up here, in all this serenity.

Speaking of serenity, I'm anything but calm. In fact, I feel almost jittery, like I'm about to close on a billion-dollar deal. In part, it's because I want Juno's family to like me, but mainly, it's because I'm going to see Juno face to face after all this time. I'm honest enough with myself to admit that.

The limo stops, and Elijah opens the door for me.

The house in front of me is small but nice, with a brand-new red tile roof and a fresh coat of white paint that makes it stand out among its neighbors. The snowboarding company her parents own is clearly doing well.

I grab the gifts and step onto the porch to ring the doorbell.

An attractive middle-aged woman with Juno's honey-colored eyes and bright smile opens the door.

"Hello," I say. "Juno didn't warn me she had a sister."

Corny, I know, but Elijah assured me this would win me some brownie points with the mom. Given the even brighter smile on her face, Elijah was right.

"You must be Lucius." She extends her hand.

Instead of shaking it, I kiss it—another Elijah suggestion that is spot on, at least as far as generating a blush on her face goes.

"I'm Lily," she says. "Come on in. I can see why Juno is so smitten."

More like *acting* smitten, but that's something Juno's mom can't know.

"This is for you, Lily." I hand her a bouquet of gloriosa lilies freshly delivered from Zimbabwe as I follow her into the house.

She sniffs the flowers with an ecstatic expression on her face just as a tall, silver-haired man comes up behind her and extends his hand to me. "I'm John," he says good-naturedly. "Am I interrupting your attempts to charm my wife?"

I give him a bottle of Hennessy Paradis. "If you're a fan of cognac, I think I have a better chance of charming you."

I know he is, thanks to a little homework—which

pays off, given how wide John's eyes get when he realizes what he's got. "For this, I just might let you take my wife on a date," he says with apparent seriousness.

I smile. "Juno is the only one I'll be taking out."

"Taking me where?" Juno asks, appearing from behind a corner.

Time seems to slow momentarily, like in a teen movie when the heroine dolls up for the prom and descends a staircase (even if her house is one story tall).

The urge to go up to her and pull her into my arms is beyond strong, but her parents are here. In the end, I merely give her a chaste kiss on the cheek, but even that makes me hard—an awkward position to be in with her family all around us. Seems like that business about distance making the heart grow fonder should be extrapolated to other body parts.

To get my biology under control, I quickly think of unsexy things, like dirt under fingernails, eye gunk, and politicians. Just as it's beginning to work, someone rings the doorbell.

It's an elderly couple, and they both carry trays with food.

I lean down to whisper to Juno—and end up almost licking her ear in the process. "Is this a potluck?"

"No." She darts a guilty glance at her mom. "My grandparents just like to help out."

I take out my phone and text Elijah to bring in whatever we've got in the limo fridge. If other guests are bringing food, so will I.

By the time I'm introduced to the first set of grand-parents, another elderly couple arrives—also with food.

"Should we go to the table?" John asks.

The doorbell rings.

Lily frowns. "Everyone is already here."

"That's my butler," I say.

A lot of eyebrows go up, and Juno chuckles. "Didn't I tell you he's got a butler?"

Lily looks very curious as she opens the door, revealing Elijah with a big tray.

Thanking him, she accepts the offering and says, "Why don't you join us?"

Elijah takes a step back. "Oh, I don't think it would be proper."

More eyebrows go up, probably in response to the British accent.

"Nonsense," Lily says. "You brought food; there-fore, you have to come in."

Elijah looks aghast. "This is the master's food. I merely brought it."

Lily makes puppy eyes at him. "Please? I wouldn't enjoy dinner knowing you're sitting alone in the car."

Elijah throws me a questioning glance, and I nod as imperceptibly as possible. His joining us just might save me from committing a social faux pas that would otherwise jeopardize my intent to charm this family. He, being a butler, is much better at these things. Then again, most people are better at these things than I am.

"If you so insist, it would be my honor," Elijah says

stiffly. He reaches over and takes the tray from Lily. "Where would you like me to place this?"

Lily leads him through the living room, and the rest of the family follow, except Juno.

She steps up to me and whispers conspiratorially, "Just a heads up, my mom's cooking is bad."

I look down at her, eyebrows raised. "That's not a nice thing to say."

She sighs. "I know, but once you taste her so-called cooking, you'll realize that 'bad' *was* the nicest word I could've used. 'Beyond atrocious,' 'unimaginably horrendous,' or 'crime against humanity' are more fitting, but because I love her, I showed restraint."

"Yeah," I say. "Your restraint is legendary."

She narrows her eyes. "You've been warned. Just please take a sampling of her dishes and eat some, or if you can't stomach it, at least smear the food around your plate so she can't tell. And compliment her, of course."

I peer into her gaze and instantly crave honey. "What kind of a monster do you think I am?"

She scoffs. "You know you can be blunt."

"Me, blunt? You wound me."

"It's an unwritten rule in our family to let Mom think she *can* cook. If her dishes are the only ones uneaten, she might figure out the truth."

Something occurs to me. "Is that why your grand-parents brought food?"

She nods. "The official story is that they want to

help out. That's also why my dad makes a few dishes of his own for each event. In fact, when it's not a big get-together, Dad is the one to cook."

I chuckle. "Your mom doesn't realize she's bad at it?"

Juno looks horrified at the very idea. "She thinks her food is amazing. Dad has convinced her that it's too good, and that he'd overeat and get fat if she made it all the time. So, 'for his health,' he cooks his 'inferior' dishes."

"Very cute," I say, my eyes roaming over Juno's animated features. Without meaning to, I find myself leaning toward her, my voice deepening as I murmur, "No. Beautiful."

She moistens her lips and steps a fraction closer as she whispers, "If I had a flaw, I think I'd want to know."

Should I tell her about her many flaws? Like how her lips are too tempting for my comfort? How her intelligence made it impossible not to call her this week and keep my distance as I originally wanted? Or how her heaving chest is too fucking arousing, making me—

"Juno?" her father yells from somewhere, saving me from doing something crazy, like attacking her here and now, in this hallway.

"Coming!" she yells back, then looks at me apologetically. "Ready?"

"I'll be right behind you," I say, my voice a bit hoarse.

She tells me where the bathroom is if I need it, then sashays away.

At first, I follow her, but then I decide that a stop in the bathroom would be worth it—to splash some cold water on my face.

When that move fails, I'm forced to once again think the un-sexiest thoughts in my arsenal because even if earwax and boogers aren't great for my appetite, they're better than the alternative: for Juno's parents to witness how my biology reacts to their daughter.

Chapter 29

Juno

By SAGUARO'S OVARIES, was I about to kiss Lucius again?

Maybe. I certainly wanted to, and if Dad hadn't called out, I might have. How would Lucius have reacted? For a moment, it seemed like he was flirting with me, but maybe he was just getting deeper into the role?

Ugh, I really need to keep my libido under control. In my defense, Lucius looks particularly delicious today—and I blame all the phone conversations for that.

Now that I know him better, it's hard to view him as solely a grumpy asshole. Not that he isn't that, of course—there are just so many other sides to him, including the man who loves his grandmother so much he's willing to go to incredible lengths to make her happy.

As I walk into the kitchen, I see that everyone's left the most visible 'head of the table' spots empty for us. Very subtle. If we were getting married here today, that's where we'd sit.

"Where is Lucius?" Mom asks, looking much too worried, all things considered. What does she think, that I broke up with him in the minute they left us alone? Or cannibalized him?

"He's right behind me," I say. "Probably washing his hands."

Sitting down, I examine the table.

There's enough food to feed a dorm full of hungry fraternity brothers—assuming they haven't binged on caterpillars. As usual, experience and my enhanced sense of self-preservation tell me which dishes are Mom's. Lucius's contribution also stands out: a tray of fancy little tarts with smoked fish and cream cheese, caviar on crackers, tiny crabcakes, and cucumber sandwiches along with other hors d'oeuvres. Clearly, Elijah is behind some of these selections, given how well they'd go with British afternoon tea.

"Ah, there he is," Mom says and flaps her eyelashes coquettishly at my date.

Seriously? With her husband right there? Then again, my grandmothers are also checking out Lucius admiringly. I guess he brings that out in anyone who likes males.

"Everything smells delicious," Lucius says, his lips

curving in an uncharacteristically warm smile. He throws a quick glance at Elijah, who nods approvingly.

What was that about? Did the butler coach him on how to be nice at dinner?

"Wait 'til you taste Lily's paella," Dad says and points at the dish I already suspected of having Mom's particular touch. There are anise hyssop flowers in it (used as garnish?), which will add a licorice taste where it doesn't remotely belong.

As everyone takes turns explaining what they brought, I ladle myself a little bit of everything and make a big show of getting some of Mom's paella. I'm actually curious about it. The ingredients in this dish can vary greatly, so how badly could she mess it up?

The answer: spectacularly. I put a tiny spoonful into my mouth and find it very difficult not to spit it out.

When I think of herbs and spices associated with paella, things like paprika, turmeric, oregano, garlic, pepper, rosemary, and saffron come to mind. None of those are here. What I do detect is vanilla. And nutmeg. And soy sauce, for some reason? And what's with the croutons? Oh, and let's not forget the barely cooked rice, the overcooked, rubbery seafood, and enough salt to give everyone instant hypertension.

Mom is truly a virtuoso when it comes to making food inedible. Not for the first time, I wonder if there's something wrong with her tastebuds—she munches on the paella gladly and looks like she's genuinely enjoying it.

I catch Lucius putting a forkful of the atrocity into his mouth and watch to see how good he is at hiding his reaction.

His eyes widen. His chewing becomes labored. With clear difficulty, he swallows the mouthful. Then, with great feeling, he loudly says, "Wow, Lily. This paella is out of this world."

Damn, that was good. He channeled his real emotions into that lie—which was not even a lie. This food is truly not of this world. It's what the Upside Down monsters must eat in *Stranger Things*.

Dad looks at Lucius approvingly. "As of this moment, you have my blessing if you want to marry my daughter."

"Dad!" I feel like I might fall through my chair.

"When *are* the two of you getting hitched?" Mom asks excitedly.

"Mom!" Make that fall through my chair *and* the floor.

"And when can we expect great-grandkids?" my two grandmothers ask, somehow in unison.

"Could you make one of said kids a boy?" the grandfathers chime in—also in suspicious synchrony.

"Did you rehearse this?" I ask in a choked voice. I now want to fall through the whole fucking mountain and keep going to the center of the Earth.

Lucius smirks at me. I suppose that's better than

running away screaming, which is how a real boyfriend would react to all that marriage-and-kids noise.

Hiding the smirk, Lucius faces my family and solemnly says, "Thanks, John. I'll keep your blessing in mind. For now, Juno and I aren't there just yet." He looks adoringly at me. "Right, sweetie?"

"Right, shnookums," I say. "Unholy matrimony will have to wait."

Is Mom pouting? And are my grandparents really that upset, or have they simply swallowed some paella?

Speaking of paella... Looking extremely uncomfortable at being in the middle of all this family stuff, Elijah grabs himself a plateful of my mom's dish. What a huge mistake.

Lucius eyes his butler with pity, as do all the members of my family who aren't Mom. However, as soon as Mom looks his way, Lucius's expression changes to that of curiosity, and he asks her how she and Dad met.

Wow. If it was Elijah who suggested that icebreaker, he deserves a raise—or to be saved from that paella. Left to his own devices, Lucius would've probably asked Mom some crazy question from that online list—like what type of clown she would like to eat.

Mom's face becomes animated as she launches into the story of their meet-cute. She and Dad are childhood sweethearts, so their treacle tale starts back in middle school.

Because I've heard the story a million times, I tune it out and watch Elijah instead.

With great confidence, the butler shovels the first spoonful into his mouth.

As the paella assaults his poor tastebuds, his pupils dilate, and his face turns a greenish hue.

To Elijah's credit—or that of his butler school—he doesn't otherwise show his distaste. He just swallows the mouthful with a micro-expression that reminds me of how children take pills.

He chews the next spoonful in a style reminiscent of a camel. That doesn't seem to help much. The torment is still noticeable on his face if you're looking for it. Then, with the mien of a man headed for the gallows, he takes another spoonful, and another.

He must want the pain to be over with quickly. Makes sense. I would've done that in his shoes—assuming I couldn't sneak some paella into my purse.

In the valiant fight against the paella, Elijah comes out the victor—and for the rest of the meal, he sticks exclusively to the items he brought from the limo.

Chapter 30

Lucius

"WE HOPE to see you again soon," Lily gushes as she kisses my cheeks, first one, then the other.

I tolerate the display of affection, though usually, my instinct would be to pull away. In general, to my surprise, the entire dinner was quite tolerable. Maybe even nice. The warm family atmosphere, the gentle ribbing, the way they pretended to like Lily's terrible cooking—it all made me a little wistful. True, I've experienced some of this with Gram, but she's only one woman and can't create such a festive atmosphere all by herself.

Maybe I'll make myself a big family like that one day.

Wait, what am I thinking?

"We should leave them alone," Lily says, nodding at me and then Juno. "Let them say 'goodbye.'" She puts the last word in air quotes, and Juno rolls her eyes.

"I'm not giving you a ride?" I ask Juno once everyone follows Lily's suggestion and disappears inside the house.

She shakes her head. "Mom wants me to stay overnight."

"Ah." I feel a pang of disappointment. We didn't really get a chance to interact today.

Juno nods at the door and whispers, "I'd bet my cactus they're watching us."

My heart skips a beat. Is she saying what I think she's saying? I decide that I'm going to assume so regardless.

"Well then." I put my hand on her lower back and dip my head. "Should we keep up appearances?"

She rises onto her tiptoes, her honey eyes gleaming. "Afraid so." Her warm breath whispers across my lips. "Can't let all those rehearsals go to waste."

My heart pounds faster. Not needing any more encouragement, I slant my lips over hers. It's a playful kiss at first, but quickly, our tongues are dancing in earnest. Her lips are deliciously plump and damp, and my whole body goes stiff—some parts much more than others.

Fuck. Did she just brush her small hand over my cock?

Breathing raggedly, I pull away. "I thought your family was watching."

She blinks rapidly, like she's trying to reorient

herself. Finally, she whispers, "Serves them right for being Peeping Toms."

I'm suddenly very glad she didn't accept my offer of a limo ride home. If we spend another second together, I'm not sure I'll keep my sanity.

"See you at Gram's house?" I ask hoarsely. "Unless—"

"Yeah." She steps back and dampens her lips. "What should I bring?"

Those plump, soft lips. Fucking hell. I do my best to sound normal. "Nothing. But definitely *not* any leftovers."

She grins. "You sure? I bet Gram is a fan of paella."

I shudder as I recall the taste. "Let's not make my chefs feel like their jobs aren't secure."

"Chefs, as in plural?"

"I have three. Not counting the ones who work in my restaurants."

She rolls her eyes. "I hope three is enough. I mean, what if all of them got sick at the same time? You'd starve."

"Actually, Elijah's cooking is serviceable. Same goes for all but one of my housekeepers. And in a pinch, I do know how to make mac-and-cheese or an omelet."

"Wow. With those critical life skills, you could even survive on a deserted island."

Why do I want to kiss her again? Probably to shut her up.

"When should I send a limo after you tomorrow?" I ask.

"I'll text you."

"Okay." Why am I so reluctant to leave? "Bye?"

She hesitates for a second, then blows me an air kiss before escaping into her parents' home.

———

As soon as I get home, I take care of my sexual frustration, and the session is a lot more vigorous than all the Florida post-phone-call ones.

I then take a shower, go for a run, and visit my ferrets.

The collective noun for ferrets is a 'business,' and I think whoever came up with that did so because there's always some funny business going on when it comes to ferrets, especially if there's more than one in your vicinity.

Today, for example, Caligula manages to devour the special treats I brought for everyone before Blackbeard and Malfoy so much as get a taste. I also locate the gardening gloves one or more of them managed to steal—and they're in shreds.

As I play with the little devils, I fight the urge to call Juno. After all, we've only been apart for three hours. Even if our relationship were real, it would be too soon to miss her. Unless... Maybe I should—

My phone rings.

Could this be Juno?

No.

It's Gram.

Smiling despite my disappointment, I pick up.

"Did you enjoy meeting her parents?" she asks in lieu of a hello.

I tell her all about it, minus Lily's atrocious cooking. I don't want to bias Gram in case she ever tries said cooking.

Wait. Why would she try it?

"If Juno likes me tomorrow, you're as good as married," Gram says, beyond excited.

I suppress a groan. "Please don't joke about that when you see her. Her family was saying the same thing."

"Who said I'm joking?" Gram asks.

I pinch the bridge of my nose. "Oh, no." I make my tone worried. "The ferrets are chewing through my shoes."

"Ferrets," Gram says the word like a curse. "You're still cavorting with those beasts?"

Being terrified of rats, Gram has decided that she doesn't like ferrets because "they're similarly shaped."

"Don't worry. I won't bring them with me." I make a mental note to check my pockets before I head over to her place. The last thing I want at Gram's house is a repeat of what happened at the fundraiser. She'd try to jump on a table and would probably hurt herself.

"Don't bring them," she says. "Just thinking of the

things makes me want to drink some chamomile tea to calm down."

"You go do that," I say with a smile. "Maybe have some valerian root as well."

"Good idea. Bye."

I hang up and notice that the ferrets are looking at me with strange expressions on their mischievous faces.

"Sorry about that," I say to them. "Your great-grandma didn't mean to be mean."

———

As I head to bed, I have the strongest urge to call, or at least text, Juno. I recently discovered there's such a thing as a cactus emoji—and I bet if I used it, she'd swoon.

But no. Bad idea.

My priority is to get good sleep so I'm on my very best behavior when Juno and I finally present the fartlek to Gram.

Chapter 31

Juno

As THE LIMO Lucius sent after me pulls up to Lucius's grandma's house—which is really a small mansion—my stomach feels like a blooming cactus being swarmed by butterflies.

Yesterday's combination of Lucius and my family made the line between fake and real boyfriend blurrier than ever, so much so I'm still having trouble reining the idiocy in. That scorching kiss aside, Lucius was amazing with my family. I don't care how much Elijah coached him—Lucius looked like he was enjoying himself, and he's not a good enough actor to fake that... I don't think.

The limo stops, and as the door opens, I come face to face with Lucius himself—which makes those pollinators in my belly go truly berserk.

"Hi." I climb out with the help of his proffered

hand, and when we touch, I feel it between my legs—a pleasant but unwelcome situation.

Releasing my hand, he turns his back to me and says, "Follow."

Just "follow?" No greeting kiss for the fake girlfriend? No hug? No "nice to see you?"

Fine. Be like that. I let him lead me inside the house, where I finally get to see his Gram.

The first thing that springs to mind is just how tiny this woman is—and this is coming from me, who's far from a giantess. The second thing: she must have laughed a lot in her life. The evidence of it is etched into the lines around her mouth and in the dimple in her cheek.

The same kind of dimple that Lucius has, I realize with a peculiar pinching in my chest.

Lucius gives her a big, warm hug and kisses her on the cheek—thus proving that he knows that greeting hugs and kisses are things people do.

Gram beams at him, and the whole situation is extremely adorable, especially since Lucius is just a few wires short of being a robot.

"Gram, this is my girlfriend, Juno," he says, making me feel like I've just received a gold medal. "Juno, this is—"

"Pearl," Gram says to me. "Call me Pearl."

I grin. "My best friend is also named Pearl."

She grins back. "I hope I'll also become your friend, just like the other Pearl."

I hope she will not overshare about sex the way the younger Pearl does—like that time my friend told me she unironically enjoys a sexual act called *a pearl necklace*.

"You weren't exaggerating," Gram says to Lucius. "She really *is* strikingly beautiful."

He looks taken aback—which makes me doubt he ever told his crafty grandmother such a thing.

I do my best to salvage the situation. "So, Pearl, do you have pictures of Lucius as a child?"

She gives me an approving look. "Going right for the jugular. I like you already."

As she leads us to the living room, Lucius whispers, "That's unfair. I didn't see such photos of you yesterday."

Pearl hands me a thick photo album, and I plop on the couch.

Lucius sits next to me. My heartbeat picks up. His large, muscular frame radiates enough heat to boil eggs... or fertilize them.

When Pearl sits on my other side, I open the album and greedily peruse it, an ear-to-ear grin splitting my face at the cuteness overload. Lucius was the most adorable kid ever, with a dimpled smile and big gray eyes. If we had a son—

No. I close the album with a loud clap and look guiltily at Pearl. "What about his teenage years?"

That should be safer, right?

She grimaces. "Unfortunately, Lucius's mother 'borrowed' that album and never returned it."

"As is typical," Lucius mutters under his breath.

Before I can comment, a burly middle-aged man walks into the room, carrying a tray with drinks.

"Ah, thank you, dear," Pearl says to him before turning to me. "This is Aleksy."

"Nice to meet you. I'm Juno," I say to Aleksy.

Aleksy sets the drinks on the coffee table. "And I you," he says, and I detect an Eastern European accent.

With a courtly bow, he leaves us be.

I ask Pearl which drink is hers and hand it to her.

"Polite, too," she says approvingly to Lucius. "Don't mess this up."

Lucius sighs. "Will you ladies excuse me for a second? I want to have a word with Aleksy."

Pearl narrows her eyes. "Why? I assure you, my sugar has been between seventy and ninety. My blood pressure is that of an athlete. No back pain still, without pills. Even my bow—"

"I'd like to hear all this from Aleksy," Lucius says firmly, standing up.

"Doesn't trust me," Pearl whispers to me so loudly that he can definitely hear.

Before Lucius can exit the room, my phone rings.

I show Pearl my phone screen. "See? That's my friend and your namesake calling." I decline the call and put my phone on the coffee table. "I'll call her back later."

Lucius shakes his head, the way he does every time he spots my not-smart-phone, and then goes off to talk to Aleksy.

As soon as he's gone, Pearl leans toward me and says in a low voice, "I'm glad you didn't take that call."

"Oh?"

Pearl's gaze locks with mine. "There's something I wanted to talk to you about without my grandson present."

My pulse speeds up. "Oh, sure. What is it?"

She hesitates for a second. "Lucius... he can be a little prickly."

I almost burst out laughing. "A *little* prickly?"

She sighs. "Is he very prickly?"

I smile sheepishly. "Well, maybe not very. At least not to me."

"Good," she says softly. "I was worried. He seems to care a lot about you."

More like he's a great actor. "We're fine."

"You don't seem to mean that," she says, cocking her head.

Damn it. Am I messing up the whole fartlek? "I guess..." I take a breath and search for something to say that would ring true to her. "Sometimes, I get the sense that he holds back. Like he's wary of getting close."

Actually, that's true, period. Not that I can blame him, given the fakeness of our relationship. I hold back myself because that's just logical.

She nods. "He is—wary, that is. I hope you can be

238

patient with him. He may be rich now, but he hasn't had an easy life. First, his useless father left him and my daughter. Then she turned out to be a less-than-ideal mother, as much as it saddens me to say it." She lets out a heavy sigh. "When things like that happen, a boy is bound to question if he's lovable—and the high school girls didn't help matters."

"High school girls?" I say dubiously. The rest of what she said I've already suspected—though my heart aches to hear it confirmed. "I would've thought high school girls swarmed Lucius like angry bees. In heat."

I know I would have, if we'd been in school together.

Pearl scrunches her face. "You'd think so, looking at him now, right? But that wasn't the case, I'm afraid. As cute as he was as a child, it was an ugly duckling situation when he was a teen. At least for a time. He got gangly overnight, and it took him a few years to grow into his body. Didn't help that he was already starting to be prickly." She sighs again. "As far as I know, he didn't start dating at all until he made big money—and now he thinks that's all any woman is interested in when it comes to him."

Of course. That would explain why his first kiss happened around the time he made his first million—and why he didn't want to elaborate on it when I asked.

"Since I can tell what the two of you have is real," Pearl continues, "I wanted to—"

Lucius strides into the room, his eyes flinty. "Of

239

course, what Juno and I have is real. But go on, what was it you wanted to do?"

"I wanted to tell Juno that you seem like the perfect couple," Pearl says—and sounds so earnest that I would believe her if I didn't know for a fact she was going to say something else. Something like "give him the benefit of the doubt."

"Try again," Lucius says.

"Fine." Pearl's eyes gleam mutinously. "I was going to tell her about your PhD in Roman history. I know you never would."

"Because it's an honorary one," he says. "Get famous or give a school a large-enough donation, and you'll get one too."

"I'm sure there's more to it than that. Have you at least told Juno about your MBA?" she asks. "You earned that, right?"

He sighs. "Juno's dream is to get a degree of her own, so I figured that bragging about my scholastic accomplishments would be gauche."

"That doesn't follow," I say. "I can be proud of you... and a little jealous at the same time. Besides, I want a degree in Botany. You don't have one of those, do you?"

"No," he and Pearl say in unison.

"Then I'm only a little jealous," I say. "And, obviously, impressed."

"See?" Pearl says. "No problem. You should have told her."

Lucius rubs his temples. "Are you trying to make me forget what I came in here to say?"

Pearl grins. "It was probably, 'Juno, I missed you.'"

"No," he says grumpily. "I was going to ask you about your elbow."

"Aleksy, you're a traitor!" Pearl yells.

"What happened?" Lucius demands.

Pearl lifts her right elbow theatrically. "Nothing. I probably overplayed badminton. Aleksy had me ice the elbow for a few days, and it's feeling better."

Lucius examines her elbow with such intensity you'd think he's x-raying it with his gaze. "You're seeing a doctor tomorrow," he announces. "I know you're up by ten, so that's when I'll have him come over."

As they gently bicker about the timing, I can't help but smile on the inside. I already knew that Lucius cared about his grandmother, but his overprotectiveness is showing me just how much—and it gives me an epiphany about him that I should have gotten much, much sooner.

If Lucius were a plant, he'd be a cactus. Prickly at first glance, but in the right circumstances—like around his grandmother—he blooms. He had a tough start in life but was able to make billions and otherwise thrive. Just like his cactus brethren, Lucius has hidden depths to him that I'm still unraveling.

This explains a lot. Like the way he's been hijacking all my thoughts lately. I mean, I love cactuses, so should it be so surprising that—

Aleksy walks in the room. "The chefs are here with the dinner."

———

At dinner, Pearl turns into a hybrid between an inquisitor and a detective, so all our earlier get-to-know-each-other training pays off in spades. What impresses me the most is how many details Lucius remembers about me—even things I mentioned in passing.

It's nice to be noticed like that, even if it's just to fool his grandmother today.

"Have you heard from your mother?" Pearl asks Lucius as we finish the divine éclairs the pastry chef made for dessert.

He nods. "Your daughter is on a safari in Botswana."

"Ah." Pearl dabs her mouth with a napkin. "Excuse me a moment. I have to go powder my nose."

As soon as she leaves, Lucius whispers, "I bet this is a test."

I raise an eyebrow. "What kind?"

"To see if we'll be able to keep our hands off each other."

Is he saying what I think he's saying? I swallow the last bit of éclair over a lump in my throat. "Did you want to put our earlier practice to use?"

He looks at my lips greedily. "If she catches us, it will cement the fartlek."

Grr. I'm beginning to really, really hate that f-word.

"Unless you mind?" he says.

Saguaro give me strength. I turn to him and pucker my lips. "Let's do it."

He leans in, and our lips lock.

Oh, my. He tastes of chocolate and vanilla from the éclair, but also like him—deliciously male.

If this is purely a performance on his part, it's good. My nipples are certainly giving it a standing ovation, and my ovaries whistle and catcall.

"Couldn't wait, could you?" Pearl's tone is the opposite of judgey, but I feel like a naughty teen anyway.

I pull away, and my heart skips a beat at the heat in Lucius's eyes. Can he fake that? Also, is that a tent under the napkin on his lap, or am I seeing things?

"Sorry," I say to his grandmother sheepishly. "I confused Lucius's mouth for an éclair."

Ugh, why did I say that? There's something much more X-rated that's éclair-shaped under that napkin.

"It's quite all right, dear," Pearl says. "Dessert isn't complete without a kiss from one's sweetheart."

"Gram," Lucius says with mock-sternness. "Don't make Juno feel awkward."

She chuckles. "Are you sure it's Juno who feels awkward?"

Lucius puts his hands in a prayer position. "Can we please talk about something else?"

Oh, no. The eyes he's making at his grandmother. If he ever used that look on me, I'd say yes to pretty much anything. Particularly dirty anything.

"Okay," Pearl says graciously. "Will you leave the leftovers when you go?"

Lucius shakes his head. "I think I'd better take the dessert with me, so you're not tempted."

They argue about the fate of the dessert for a few minutes as I sip my non-caffeinated tea. Then Pearl launches into a story about fighting for women's rights in her youth.

As I listen, I can't help but feel a gnawing sense of dread. Will Lucius and I stop spending time together now that his grandmother is utterly fooled into thinking that we're together?

No. It's too soon for that.

Still, we have an expiration date.

It hadn't hit me until now just how much I don't want whatever it is between us—no matter how fake—to end. I like kissing my human cactus. I like talking on the phone with him. And having dinners with him.

Is it possible he feels something similar? If so, how would I go about finding that out?

"Juno?" Lucius's voice intrudes into my thoughts, and I sit up with a start.

"Yes?" What did I miss?

He smirks. "The question was, are you ready

244

to go?"

"Go?"

He nods at Pearl. "It's Gram's bedtime."

She rolls her eyes. "I can stay up later."

I leap to my feet. "No, no, I'm ready. Sorry about the woolgathering."

"It's understandable." Pearl gives me a lascivious wink. "It is getting late."

What is this grandmother implying? Whatever it is, my cheeks burn. Traitors.

To make matters worse, Lucius puts his hand on my lower back to lead me out. My cheeks burn hotter and my brain short-circuits. On autopilot, I tell Pearl what a great pleasure it was to meet her, and she returns the sentiment. I think.

Keeping his hand on me, Lucius leads me to the limo and shepherds me inside.

"Great job," I say when his touch is gone and coherent thoughts return. "She has to think we're really together."

He agrees, but all I can think is that Pearl isn't the only one fooled. The way he looks at me—I'm not sure what's real anymore... and that makes a crazy idea invade my mind.

A way to see if I'm alone in my confusion, or if Lucius might be in the same yacht.

The idea is simplicity itself, but I'm not sure if I have the proverbial balls to carry it out.

All I need to do is invite Lucius over to my place.

245

Chapter 32

Lucius

As the limo pulls away from Gram's house, I position my legs to hide the hard-on that's been bothering me all evening. Until today, I thought "blue balls" was something teenage boys invented to get their reluctant girlfriends to give them hand jobs, but now I'm on the verge of acquiring the mythical condition myself.

"Lucius?" I hear Juno say as if from a distance.

"Yes?"

She chews on her lip. "There's something I wanted to ask you."

I give her half of my attention while the other half is working on a list of gross things in order to calm my overactive biology. Her lip chewing isn't helping.

"Never mind," she says after a beat.

Now she's got my full attention. "Something to do with Gram?"

She shakes her head. "I was just... Never mind."

She's usually a lot more eloquent than that. Maybe it's a food coma?

"Do you mind if I check my email then?" I ask her. It's an unsexy activity that might help calm down my dick.

"Go for it," she says, but she looks extremely disappointed. "In fact, I should call back Pearl—my friend, the cat owner. Not your grandmother." She taps her pockets, then rummages in her purse, her expression more worried by the second.

"Did you lose your antique?" I ask.

She nods, but then her eyes light up. "I think I left it on the coffee table at your grandmother's house."

"Ah, makes sense."

"Can we go get it?" she asks. "I might get calls from my clients and—"

"Sure," I say, then lower the partition and tell Elijah to turn around.

Juno suddenly looks uneasy. "Wait. Isn't your grandmother sleeping by now?"

I shrug. "I have the keys."

———

"Let's sneak in quietly so we don't wake Gram," I tell Juno as I open the door.

She nods, and we tiptoe into the house and down the corridor.

As we approach the living room, I hear something I

can't quite make sense of. The sound is like someone slowly clapping their hands.

Shit. A surge of concern makes me speed up, leaving Juno behind.

A frantic heartbeat later, I enter the living room—just as the clapping is joined by two blood-chilling sounds.

A male grunt and a female moan.

I gape at the scene in front of me, my brain refusing to comprehend what my eyeballs are seeing.

A naked Aleksy is sprawled on the couch, his hands tied with a thick rope to the coffee table that was our destination. But that's not the part that's crashing my brain's operating system.

That honor belongs to the person riding the body-guard as if he were a rodeo bull.

Gram.

Chapter 33

Juno

I DIDN'T KNOW a neck could go pale, but Lucius's does based on something he's seeing inside the living room.

My first scary thought is that something has happened to Pearl, but then I hear the sounds.

Oh, boy. Is that what I think it is?

Reaching Lucius's side, I stop, my eyes going wide as my cheeks catch fire.

Yep. It is indeed what I suspected.

Pearl is having her way with Aleksy—and if her moans of his name are anything to go by, she's having a blast. Oh, and despite being tied up, her bodyguard is clearly doing this consensually. His happy grunts and the "yes, mistress, yes!" are a testament to that.

My face flames hotter with embarrassment, and I can't even imagine how Lucius is feeling. Pearl's back is to us, but I'm not sure that makes it any easier on Lucius's psyche. If I saw *my* grandparents doing it, I'd almost certainly be traumatized—even if it didn't look like a scene out of *Fifty Shades*.

Fighting a hysterical giggle, I touch Lucius's shoulder.

He jumps and whips his head toward me, his eyes wild and confused. I nod at the hallway from which we came and make the two-fingers-walking gesture.

A spark of sanity returns to his gaze. He grabs my hand, and we tiptoe away like two thieves.

Once outside, Lucius sprints to the limo as though he's being chased by horny werewolves, and since he's still clutching my hand in a death grip, I sprint with him.

"We need to go," he shouts at Elijah. "Now!"

As soon as Elijah slams on the gas, I close the privacy partition.

"Are you okay?" I ask breathlessly. Thankfully, the urge to giggle like a little girl has faded, so I can focus on Lucius instead of on how mortifying that encounter was.

"I'm not sure," he replies, sounding dazed. "I mean, I'm happy that she's healthy enough to do that, but..." He shakes his head. "Sorry. I'm not sure I want to talk more about this."

"Good idea." I myself would like to have these recent images expunged from my memory, so I bet he'd pay a billion for that memory wipe treatment from *Eternal Sunshine*. "Just one last tangentially related thing—my phone."

"Right," he says. "I'll get it tomorrow."

I fight the urge to kiss the crease on his forehead. "Will you tell either of them that you know?"

"Never," he says with feeling.

Okay. I owe him a change of subject, big time, so I say, "Tell me what your favorite feature of Novus Rome will be."

I'm officially a billionaire whisperer. His face returns to its normal hue, the crease relaxes, and his eyes brighten. "It's hard to pick just one favorite. Have I told you about our smart mobility plan?"

I think he has, but I shake my head since this is more of a therapy situation, not information gathering on my part.

He proceeds to tell me that Novus Rome will not allow residents to keep their cars inside the community. Those who own personal cars will have to leave them in a parking lot outside Novus Rome. Inside, a fleet of self-driving electric cars will be the transportation of choice. No need for private garages, no air pollution, and everyone will be much safer since said cars will always follow the speed limit and communicate with each other and the roads in order to avoid any and all accidents.

"Wait," I say, intrigued despite myself. "Novus Rome will have sensors in the sidewalks and roads?"

He nods excitedly.

"Sounds Orwellian," I say.

He shrugs. "The data will only be used for car navigation and pedestrian safety."

"Huh, okay. What's your second-favorite feature?"

He talks about the superfast internet access everyone in Novus Rome will enjoy for free, even while hiking in the preserved woods.

Usually, I'd question the wisdom of having people plugged in like that when they're trying to enjoy nature, but the limo stops, and my earlier goal of inviting him over to my place resurfaces its horny head, causing me to get tongue-tied once again.

"We're here." He gestures out the window, his expression unreadable.

"Yeah." I know I should go, but I don't move, not even when Elijah opens the door.

Worse yet, my cheeks flush, despite the fact that I haven't said anything, let alone invited anyone anywhere.

Gah.

Since when am I such a scaredy cat? Why can't I be bold, like his grandmother, who clearly asked a much younger man if she could tie him up before—

"I'll walk you to your door," Lucius states.

"Thanks," I blurt and finally move my ass out.

This is good. I have more time to summon my courage.

Except the whole walk to my place, I'm as silent as a Charlie Chaplin movie. Finally, there's no more walk to be had, at which point I deliver my best conversational gambit to date: "This is a door. I mean, my door."

The corners of his eyes smile. "I'm familiar with the concept of a door. Yours sounds special."

I bite my lip. "You've probably designed some sort of smart door for the houses in Novus Rome. A door that probably greets you and opens on its own." And maybe such a door would be able to invite fake boyfriends in when the owner is a chicken.

He moistens his lips—though it looks a bit like a wolf licking his chops. "That's a great idea. I haven't given smart doors much thought just yet."

Shit. He looks like he wants to kiss me. Or is that wishful thinking on my part?

I suck in a calming breath. This is it. I'm going to get him inside. "My Murphy bed is stuck. Can you help?" I rattle out in one breath—just as he also says something.

"What did you say?" I ask, mentally chastising myself. Why Murphy bed? What was I thinking? Being in my bedroom, that's way too brazen and obvious. Also, how do I now fake it being stuck?

"I asked if I could see your cactus again," Lucius says. "I didn't know how important it was to you when you gave me that tour. What was it you said? Something about Murphy's Law?"

A huge, silly grin bursts out on my face. "Don't worry about what I said. You can totally see my cactus."

As I fumble with my keys, I can't help wondering if "cactus" is code for something else. If so, the scientific name for butterfly pea—the plant that makes that nice blue tea—would work much better, since it's Clitoria Ternatea, or simply Clitoria. Since Lucius is into Latin, he'd like that.

"There," I say when the door is open wide. "Come inside."

Damn it. Why does everything I say sound dirty all of a sudden?

He steps inside, strides over to El Duderino, and examines him very intently, seemingly with great appreciation.

Dude. Is this dude planning to munch on me? That'd be totally uncool.

"This is a beavertail, right?" Lucius asks.

All my dirty mind hears is "beaver" and then "tail," but I mumble something in the affirmative. Then I realize Lucius must've researched my cactus.

Argh! My ovaries may just explode.

Before I can think better of it, I stumble over to my Murphy bed and shake it hard enough for the springs to creak. "Oh, no. It's stuck. Can you help me?"

Damn it. Why couldn't I come up with something new?

It doesn't matter, though.

He turns, and there's heat in his eyes as he says, "Isn't that your bedroom?"

I nod and shake the Murphy bed again.

Moving with smooth, athletic grace, he walks over and tugs on the front of my couch/bed.

Whoosh.

The thing has *never* converted from couch to bed that fast.

I swallow, looking up at him. "I must have loosened that up for you."

Loosened up? What's next, discussion of lubing the gears?

He looks at the bed, then back down at me. "Goodnight?"

Damn. His voice is as husky as a purebred from Siberia. My heart hammers so fast I'm in danger of my ribcage breaking. He's staring at me with those steel-colored eyes that are beginning to look like molten metal, and I can't seem to draw in enough air. Or rather, every breath I pull in makes me acutely aware of his subtle masculine scent and the heat radiating from his large body.

"Juno…" His voice is even huskier. "I'm going to kiss you. If you don't want this, say it now."

"I…" I lick my dry lips. "I definitely want this."

And with that, I rise up on my tiptoes, wind my arms around his neck, and press my lips to his.

Chapter 34

Lucius

JUST LIKE THAT, biology wins not only the battle but the war.

Juno's soft lips are delicious, her adroit tongue maddening. I want her more than anything I've ever wanted in my life.

Greedily, I inhale her intoxicating scent—a mix of Neutrogena shampoo, Dove body wash, and something sweet that is purely Juno, the woman rightfully named after a goddess.

I pull her close, her soft parts pressing against my hardness.

She gasps delicately into my mouth, and her hands slide from my neck and down my back until one palm grabs my butt.

Damn, that feels good. If only our clothes were not in the way... No. In a second. First, I move my kiss from her lips to her alabaster neck, breathing in more of her sweet scent, tasting the softness of her tender skin.

With a moan, she tugs on my shirt, proving that we're on the same wavelength regarding the nuisance that are our clothes.

Grudgingly, I tear my lips away from her neck and step back to remove my shirt.

Maintaining the eye contact, she takes off her top and then her bra, exposing her perfectly perky breasts.

My breath catches. "Fuck." I shove my pants off. "You're amazing." To highlight my point, I take off my boxers so that she can see my rock-hard appreciation.

She stares at my cock with wide eyes. "Holy saguaro, that's big." She slides her panties down, revealing the neatly trimmed pussy that I've been wet-dreaming about all this time.

It's even better in real life.

My mouth waters as she scans my body from head to foot. "You're like a Greek statue," she breathes when her eyes meet mine again.

My answer comes out in a low growl. "And you're exactly like a Roman one. The perfect one."

With that, I gently push her onto the bed and take one pink, hard nipple into my mouth.

Fuck me. This is heaven.

"The other one is jealous," she says on a gasp.

I release that nipple and give the other one a lick. "Sorry about that. Everyone will get their turn."

Juno arches her back, fisting her hands in my hair

as I suck on the nipple in earnest until she moans. Then I run my tongue down her breast, over her delectable belly and the neat curls until I'm at the altar of the goddess.

"I'm going to kiss you," I murmur, looking up to meet her gaze. "If you don't want it—"

"I want it." She lifts her hips off the bed. "A lot."

Good. I slide my tongue over her plump, creamy folds, then gently suck on them.

A moan is my reward.

I slide my tongue over her perfect little clit.

She utters a gasp.

"Delicious," I breathe, letting my lips vibrate against the sensitive flesh.

A louder moan is proof I'm on the right track.

I flatten my tongue.

Her moans grow in volume.

I lap at the sweetness within, then slide a finger where my cock so desperately aches to be.

Fuuuck. The velvety hot smoothness nearly makes me come. Tensing my entire body to stave it off, I move the tip of my finger until I locate the little bundle of nerves exactly below where my tongue is.

"Oh," she gasps. "Please don't stop."

Not in a million years. I lick and add pressure with my finger before flattening my tongue again.

Her whole body shudders, and the walls of her pussy clench on my finger—making my throbbing cock jerk with envy.

She sits up, her wheat-colored hair mussed and eyes wild. "Lean back."

Before I can ask why, I see it—and then feel it as Juno's luscious lips wrap around my cock.

Fuck.

Fucking fuck.

This is amazing.

Mind-bogglingly so.

Except if she keeps going, I'm going to explode.

With herculean effort, I pull her away.

She gives me a confused look.

"I have to be inside you," I growl.

Her eyes light with understanding. Escaping my grip, she crawls to the edge of the bed, and her luscious ass is the most erotic sight ever. As are her small, perfect feet, all pink and delicately feminine.

She turns back, and I realize she wasn't putting on a show for me. She's procured a condom, which she hands to me with a pretty blush.

Fucking biology. For the first time in my life, I've had zero thought of using protection. Thank fuck one of us has some brain cells still active.

Ripping the packet with my teeth, I sheathe myself as she lies on her back. Hungrily, I rake my gaze over her.

"Beautiful." The word comes out as a grunt, but in my defense, the tsunami of blood surging to my cock has robbed me of the power of speech.

Covering her small body with my much-larger one,

I dip my head to capture Juno's lips in another kiss and carefully guide the tip of my cock to her entrance. Nibbling on her earlobe, I whisper, "Ready?"

"Please," she begs.

What is she doing to me?

Using what shreds of willpower I have remaining, I enter her in a slow, sensual thrust—and feel like I've arrived home after being away for a decade. She moans, clenching her inner muscles, and I grit my teeth, holding still to let her get used to me.

When her body softens and relaxes, I press deeper, relishing how tight she is, how warm. How perfectly made for me.

My next thrust is harder, bolder. She pushes on my back to urge me on, and I quicken my pace until a moan of pleasure is wrenched from her lips.

I speed up further.

Her moans grow louder.

My balls tighten. I'm on the verge, but I fight it until she shudders under me and cries out my name.

And then I'm lost.

Her pussy squeezes me in a soft, wet vise, and I come with a groan, the pleasure bursting through my nerve endings with a violence that makes my vision blur.

Chapter 35

Juno

I'm floating in a post-orgasmic cloud of hazy contentment when strong arms lift me.

Hmm. I'm being carried somewhere. Before I find the energy to ask where, the destination becomes apparent.

The shower.

Setting me onto my feet on the tile floor, Lucius turns on the water, then lightly pushes on my butt so I step in. Once I do, he joins me.

Holy saguaro. He begins to lather me up with body wash, his strong hands roaming all over me, stroking and massaging every part of my body. I should be completely wrung out—and I am—yet somehow, he's reawakening my desire.

By the time he switches focus to himself, I'm aching with need, and by the time we're toweling off,

I'm as turned on as I was before we entered my apartment.

Biting my lip, I regard him through wet lashes. "Will I be using my own legs to get back or...?"

His lips twitch, and he bends to swing me into his arms, pressing me tightly against his hard-muscled chest as he begins walking. He doesn't seem to exert any effort as he carries me, either.

Those sexy muscles aren't just for show.

"I could get used to this, you know," I say after he lays me on the bed.

A cocky smirk dances on his lips. "You enjoyed yourself?"

I stretch, feeling like a cat. A well-fed, well-stroked cat. "When I came the second time, my toes curled so hard my feet hurt."

He stares at my feet, and his earlier smile is replaced with a downright carnivorous expression. "Do you want them massaged?"

I could remind him about the time I admitted to enjoying that particular act, but instead, I blurt, "Does a cactus inhale carbon dioxide at night?"

He sits on the edge of the bed and takes my right foot into his hands. His voice is husky again. "I assume that is a yes."

I start to answer, but he squeezes my foot near the toes and I exhale in pleasure instead.

Encouraged, he presses more firmly, and then his

fingers slowly traverse the distance to my ankle, bringing pleasurable relaxation in their wake.

He starts to make small circles on the arch of my foot.

I close my eyes, now feeling like a cat being petted.

He moves his thumbs up and down my Achilles tendon.

If humans could purr, I would.

When he starts to squeeze and then pull on each of my toes, I sigh in delight as I get a flashback to my earlier orgasm—especially when he starts to slide his fingers up and down each toe.

"This is the best foot massage I've ever gotten," I breathe, opening my eyes to catch his gaze. "Not a hint of tickling, I love it."

His carnivorous smile returns. "Let's see if you like this. Don't peek. Just feel."

Intrigued, I close my eyes again.

Wow. There's an intensely pleasant sensation coming from my big toe—a combo of warmth, wetness, pressure, and light suction.

It's vaguely akin to when my nipple is sucked, and even echoes in my core in a similar way.

Unable to help myself, I open my eyes.

As I figured, he's sucking on my toe.

Then he licks it, sending a bolt of heat straight to my clit.

I gasp.

He slides his tongue over the arch of my foot.

I can't help but moan.

He restarts his ministrations with my other foot, and I find my hand sliding between my thighs, pressing against the empty ache pulsing there.

"That's right," he growls, his eyes flaring. "Come for me like that."

Gladly.

My breath speeding up, I press harder on my clit as he sucks my next toe, and as he switches his attentions to the third toe, I come with a choked cry.

"Good girl," he murmurs, regarding me with molten eyes. "Are you ready for another round?"

Another round of what? I look down and gape at the throbbing erection he's sporting.

How can it look even bigger than the first time? And how can he be ready again? None of my exes had this short of a refractory period.

Does he like my feet *this* much?

Whatever the reason for the recuperation, there's a compliment in there somewhere.

I crawl to get the condom as fast as my jellied bones allow, and then I hand it to him.

"Get on all fours," he orders, stroking his massive erection.

I gleefully obey, and in an eyeblink, he's entering me again, gently at first, then more assuredly as I adjust to him.

His first deep thrust makes my eyes roll into the back of my head. After the second one, I ball my fists in the sheets, a fresh tension building in my core. He picks up his pace, thrusting harder and faster, until the tension threatens to overflow.

"Come for me," he rasps, and his hips piston into me, wrenching moans from my lips.

Just as I'm on the edge, he grabs my feet, squeezing them with just the right pressure—and I come with a scream, my toes curling under his strong fingers.

"Fuck," he grunts as I feel his release, which gives me a little aftershock orgasm of my own.

———

Drained, I drop onto the bed, my eyes closed and my body limp.

It's official. I'm ruined for all other men—and that's before he takes me back to the shower and treats me to another sensual washing.

When we're back in bed, he arranges me in a spooning position, then wraps his arms around me and breathes into the back of my neck.

This is nice.

No. Nice doesn't cut it.

This is bliss.

I sigh contentedly. In this moment, it's very easy to imagine this thing between us working out—and without any heartache. The outside world already thinks that we're together, so we would just need to change a few little labels, right? And let's be honest...

For me, the adjustment will be minuscule, thanks to all the things I've been feeling that I wasn't supposed to.

The big question is: is he on the same page?

His actions tonight strongly point in that direction, especially how tenderly he's holding me right now. Yet a chilly worry spreads through my veins. He's still a gorgeous billionaire, and I'm a small business owner who sometimes misreads the labels on boxes of fertilizer.

What if tonight was just about getting laid for him? What if he's not viewing it as a momentous occasion, but a momentary lapse of reason?

The longer I lie there, the more worried I get.

Suddenly, he pulls his arms away.

Does he need the bathroom or something?

He removes his whole body, leaving my back feeling cold.

Confused and concerned, I turn over.

Lucius is sitting on the edge of the bed, looking uncomfortable.

I sit up. "What are you doing?"

"Going home." Not meeting my gaze, he jumps to his feet and starts hunting for his clothes. "You'll want the bed for yourself."

What the hell?

I realize he might have a million-dollar pillow waiting for him at home, but I thought—

"Sorry," he says, pulling on his clothes faster than I thought humanly possible.

I narrow my eyes. "Sorry about what?"

He spreads his hands. "We shouldn't have done this."

My heart drops. "By 'we,' do you mean 'I?' And by 'this,' do you mean 'me?'"

He pulls up his zipper. "What?"

"Nothing." I fight violent urges, as well as a pressure behind my eyes. "Since you're so eager to leave, fucking leave."

"I'm not—never mind. I'm going." He puts on his shoes. "Sorry, again. Call you tomorrow?"

"Don't." He should thank saguaro I don't have a lamp nearby, or something else I could toss at his stupid head.

He gives me an indecipherable look, then closes the door with a loud bang.

I bury my face in my pillow and begin to cry.

Chapter 36

Lucius

On the way home, I battle a million questions and an increasing sense of confusion.

What have I done?

Why did I fuck her?

Why did I leave?

I've ruined everything. I let biology rule me, and now I don't know where we stand.

Fucking fuck.

This was the best sex of my life, but I have no idea if it was the same for her.

Probably not. I bet she was just playing along with this fantasy we've built.

If I weren't in a limo, I'd start pacing, but as is, I just clench and unclench my fists.

I've never been in a situation where I liked a woman this much. Never allowed myself to be.

Oh, who am I kidding? I more than like her. And

this is all fake. At least it's supposed to be fake. Only it's no longer fake on my part.

Maybe I shouldn't have left. But if I'd stayed, kept her in my arms a second longer, I would have fallen deeper into the fantasy. If I'd given in to the illusion, told myself she could care for me as much as I care for her, I'd come to regret it, I just know it. It would be like that time in high school when Amanda pretended to like me to make her ex jealous. Afterward, she acted like I was a leper.

The more I think about it, the more I doubt Juno truly feels anything for me. No amount of money can change who I am, and no woman has ever been interested in that guy. I know Juno well enough to realize that she doesn't care about money in the stereotypical gold-digger way—all she wants is to pay her tuition and have the basics needed to survive. But I also know her well enough to see just how amazing she is—and what are the chances someone like that would be the first woman to want me for anything besides the billions?

At some point, I realize that I've managed to get home and finish my bedtime routine without even noticing, like the robot I no longer wish to become. Not unless my robot body could allow me to experience what I felt earlier today, when Juno was in my arms.

Whatever. I don't need to think about robotics tonight, or about anything, really.

What I should do is try the impossible.

Falling asleep.

———

I wake up, which is odd because I didn't think I'd fall asleep with all that tossing, turning, and obsessing about Juno.

Maybe I should call her? See how badly I—

Wait.

She forgot her phone at Gram's house.

Leaping off the bed, I frantically get ready.

I promised Juno I'd get her the phone back today, so that's what I intend to do.

———

When I walk into Gram's house, Aleksy greets me with a warm smile.

Fuck. I was planning to pretend I didn't see anything and don't know anything, but I now realize that's not who I am.

"Let's speak outside for a second," I tell him sternly.

Arching an eyebrow, he follows me out.

"What's up?" he asks.

"Something I forgot to tell you when I hired you." I meet his gaze to illustrate just how deadly serious my next words will be. "If anyone ever hurts my grandmother in any way, I will put a multimillion-dollar bounty on that person's head."

Aleksy's features tighten, and his accent is thicker

than usual as he says, "If someone hurts her, you will not need to waste your money. I'll take care of it personally."

I study him intently, then nod. "Sounds like we have an understanding." I extend my hand, and he shakes it solemnly.

"Where is she?" I ask over my shoulder as I head back in.

"Gardening," he says approvingly.

I stop by the living room and pick up Juno's clunker of a phone, then head over to the backyard, where I catch Gram weeding.

"What do I pay your gardener for?" I ask in exasperation.

She looks up and grins. "He deals with the landscaping in front of the house. This here is my domain." With that, she climbs to her feet, dusts off her palms on her dress, and hurries over to give me a kiss on the cheek. "No hug," she warns. "Or there'll be dirt all over you."

"I'm not afraid of a little dirt." To prove it, I locate the nearest weed and give it a yank.

"Come," she says. "Let's talk in the dining room."

———

"Talk in the dining room" is, of course, code for eating breakfast together. I don't mind, and not just because I completely forgot about food this morning.

"So," Gram says, wagging her eyebrows. "How did the rest of your evening go?"

The grilled brie-and-pear sandwich suddenly tastes like Styrofoam. "It was good. Great. Usual."

She puts down her teacup. "What happened?"

Am I that transparent? "Nothing."

"Did you have a fight with Juno?" she prods. "Those things happen."

My jaw tenses. "No. I don't know."

Gram furrows her eyebrows. "What's the problem?"

"It's not a problem. It's just reality."

"What reality?" she demands.

"I like her," I say, and voicing it makes something tighten inside my chest. "A lot. Maybe more than a lot."

Gram chuckles. "Darling, I saw you together. You didn't need to tell me that."

I don't meet Gram's gaze. "I don't think she likes me, though. Not in the same way."

"Are you crazy?"

I blink, startled, and look at Gram.

She sighs and lays her hand over mine. "Listen. Like I just said, I saw you together—and that girl is head over heels for you."

"It was just an act." The words taste bitter in my mouth.

She scoffs. "Not an act. It's a fact. Trust me, I'm never wrong about these things."

I absentmindedly pick up my sandwich and take a big bite.

Could Gram be right?

I replay all my interactions with Juno—the date-like meals, the plane ride, Gainesville, the phone calls, meeting each other's families, and then that transcendental sex yesterday. And maybe it's my blood sugar stabilizing, but I'm starting to feel more hopeful.

At the very least, Juno seems to want me in bed. Her actions yesterday proved that much. Maybe not as much as I want her, but it's a start.

Maybe if I apply myself, I can make her want me more.

Make her love me.

I drop the unfinished sandwich onto the plate as an idea solidifies in my mind.

Why didn't I think of this sooner?

I will make Juno mine. I'll approach her like I do any business deal: with fortitude and determination. I will do whatever it takes to make what we have real.

Yes. This can work.

Maybe I acted like an idiot yesterday, but I can fix that.

I will fix everything.

Without meaning to, I jump to my feet.

Gram arches an eyebrow. "Leaving already?"

I pat the phone in my pocket. "I gotta go see about a girl. Or in this case, a Roman goddess."

Chapter 37

Juno

I WAKE up to the smell of Lucius on my sheets and an ache in my chest.

Jackknifing to my feet, I rip the offending linens off the bed and toss them into a pile. If I want to stay sane, I'll have to do emergency laundry.

When does the laundromat open again?

I reach for my phone so I can call the place, but then I recall that I forgot the stupid phone.

Ugh, I need to get it back.

My new destination—Lucius's grandmother's house.

———

A few seconds after I not-so-gently bang on Pearl's door, Aleksy opens it.

"You just missed him," he says without preamble.

Grr. "Him" must be Lucius. I didn't realize I was risking bumping into him.

Or maybe I did realize it.

Maybe I wanted it.

No.

Unlike Aleksy, I'm not a masochist.

"I forgot my phone on the coffee table in the living room," I say, and blush as I recall what else that table was involved in.

Aleksy opens the door and gestures for me to come in. I rush in quickly, praying to saguaro I don't run into Pearl. The last thing I want is to cry again if she asks me anything to do with her robot of a grandson—that wouldn't be good.

Not at all.

"The phone isn't here," I say to Aleksy, looking around the room.

He shrugs.

"Did Lucius take it?" I ask.

He scratches his chin. "It's possible."

I exhale in frustration. "Where do you think he is?"

Another shrug. "Work?"

Right. Of course. The only thing he really cares about.

Stomach tightening as I anticipate *that* encounter, I nonetheless head out to my new destination.

————

I step into the fateful building where I first saw Lucius.

The lobby is just as I remember it—a wannabe Ancient Rome museum.

Crap. Why didn't I dress to impress? It might've made Lucius regret being such an asshole, but more importantly, it would be nice to fit in with all the stylish worker drones for a change.

I feel a chill down my spine that is only partially related to the overzealous AC.

To calm myself, I approach the green wall and locate the star cactus there. "Hey, little guy," I croon. "Are you being taken care of by whoever got that job I didn't get?"

After a quick soil check, the answer seems to be yes. Good. Not *everything* is shitty in this awful universe.

Turning to the security desk, I spot the same guard who checked my ID the last time. I head over to him.

"Juno," he says excitedly. "You've made me a celebrity around here."

I blink at him. "How?"

He grins. "I got the credit for meeting you before the big boss did."

Ah. I guess that makes sense. The fact that their stone-hearted asshole of a "big boss" got a human girlfriend is probably an event of mythical proportions, and anyone involved is the gossip lottery winner.

"Is he here?" I ask, not bothering to sound like a

caring girlfriend in the slightest. "He has something I need."

"Let me check." The guard begins making calls and gets transferred a few times before he says, "Yes. Juno is here looking for—"

He stops midbreath, and I can picture Lucius on the other end. *She's stalking me now? How annoying.*

"Yes," the guard says after a beat. "I'll ask her to wait for you." Hanging up, he looks at me with slight confusion. "That was Ms. Avalin. She wants to talk to you."

"Who?"

He types a few keystrokes and turns his screen to me to show me a picture. "Her."

Ah. He's talking about Eidith. She of the extra 'i.'

Is Lucius sending her down with my phone so that he doesn't have to bother facing me himself? Or is he too busy now that he's literally and figuratively fucked me?

I wait, shifting from foot to foot, until the blond ice queen clickety-clacks over to us, hips swaying like a sexy pendulum.

"Juno," she says. "I've been hoping we could talk."

That's odd. She doesn't seem to have my phone. All she's holding is a piece of paper.

"Come," she says in a voice that indicates she's used to being obeyed.

Curious, I follow her to the nearest elevator. We get inside, but she doesn't press any buttons. After a moment, the doors close anyway and she says, "We have to make it quick."

"Make what quick?"

She sighs. "Look... I know about you and Lucius."

My stomach drops. Did he confide in her about last night?

No. That would be too much, even for him.

Best to play it cool, as hard as it is. "Can you please clarify?"

"I saw the contract on Lucius's desk. You and Lucius are not real," she says. "It's all about money for you. And there's nothing wrong with that. If anything—"

"Why do you care?" The words come out a touch hysterical.

She hands me the paper she's been holding. "That's double what he promised you."

I stare at the number on the check—which is what the paper is—in stupefied incomprehension.

"That money is yours," Eidith says. "If, and only if, you break off the fake relationship, as of today." She points at the check. "There's an email address I wrote on the back. It's that of a respected journalist. He'll expect to hear from you."

"Why?" I ask numbly.

Is she doing this on Lucius's behalf?

She shrugs. "Your arrangement has never sat right with me. If he'd asked me, I would've advised him against it."

"Oh?"

I've changed my mind about who the biggest asshole in the world is. Lucius will have to give up that title to her.

"Why do *you* care?" she asks.

Why indeed? I throw out a wild guess. "Do you want him to date you?" At her slight flinch, I press my advantage. "I bet dating you for real would be a lot like fake-dating you."

She narrows the icicles that are her eyes. "Lucius and I make a lot more sense than a billionaire and a nobody who doesn't know how to dress or act. A barely literate nobody who—"

Sucking in a sharp breath, I jam at the "door open" button.

If I stay in this elevator a moment longer, I'll hurt this bitch, badly—and since she has lawyers and witnesses who saw us go in together, I'll end up in jail.

No, thanks. I'll pass.

As soon as the doors open, I leap out, but Eidith sends a parting shot at my back. "You've been a stain to his reputation."

I almost turn back and risk jail.

But no. She'd love that.

Ripping up the check, I run out of the stupid building, jump into a cab, and put all of my effort into not embarrassing myself by crying. I feel as if Eidith has stuck a finger into the gaping wound of insecurities that Lucius opened up last night—and then made a come-hither motion, followed by a poke.

As I approach my front door, I see Lucius waiting there.

My heartbeat skyrockets.

Gulping in a calming breath, I storm over and angrily clear my throat.

He turns and looks me up and down. "There you are. I was—"

"Where's my phone?" I ask as cuttingly as I can.

Frowning, he pulls it out of his pocket. "Here. Can we—"

"No. Whatever else you want, the answer is *hell no*." I snatch the phone from his grasp and open the door.

"Do not call. Do not email. Do not text. Do not come over again," I rattle out in one shaking breath. "I never, ever want to see or hear from you again."

Chapter 38

Lucius

WHAT THE FUCK? After delivering that horrible soliloquy, Juno slams the door in my face so hard that if my nose had been an inch closer, I'd look like a pug right now.

Shit. I knew she'd be upset, but that was something else. That was more violent than I expected. And she didn't give me a chance to say what I came to say.

I knock.

She doesn't answer.

I ring the doorbell.

Same result.

I call her so-called phone.

It goes straight to voicemail.

I shout her name, loudly, but there's no response.

I doubt it will make her calmer if I break this door, even though it's tempting.

No. For now, I'll give her a chance to cool off, and then we'll talk.

I'll make sure of it.

———

When I stride into my building, everyone steps out of my way, no doubt picking up on my foul mood.

Then, to my surprise, one of the security guys shouts, "Sir?"

I look at the fellow.

Nope. Have never spoken to him in my life. I forget names but not faces. Is this an attempt at a promotion or something? I'm never in the mood for those, but especially not now.

"Did Juno find you?" the guy yells.

And just like that, he's got my undivided attention.

I nearly knock down a few of my minions on the way to the security desk, where I demand, "What do you mean by that?"

He pales. "She was here. Looking for you. She spoke to Ms. Avalin and then ran off." He looks around furtively and then adds, "Juno looked upset."

Eidith spoke to Juno? What the hell for?

I resist the urge to grab the guard by his collar. "What did they talk about?"

He shrugs. "They didn't talk here."

"Where then?"

Something in my expression makes him turn even paler. "I don't know. They took the elevator."

I join him behind the desk. "Pull up the security cameras."

He does, and we watch as the two women walk to the nearest elevator.

"Pull up the feed from that car," I order.

After Juno and I got stuck, I had all the elevators equipped with cameras, microphones, and a two-way speaker. A special team now watches and listens to those feeds at all times, and if someone gets stuck, their job is to get the situation resolved.

It feels like it takes forever, but finally, I see the recording on the screen... and hear every word Eidith said.

"You're promoted as of today," I say curtly to the guard. "But if I learn that you mentioned this to anyone, I'll make sure you don't work anywhere ever again."

He nods, eyes bugging out.

I grit my teeth and stride to the executive suites.

———

"What the fuck?" I say to Eidith instead of a hello.

"Excuse me?" She stands up, the very picture of innocence.

"Your elevator conversation was not private. You have two seconds to explain yourself."

She blanches, then lifts her chin. "What am I supposed to explain?"

"You mean besides the fact that you snooped in my desk? How about you tell me why you'd dare pay my girlfriend to break up with me?"

She's almost translucent now. "What girlfriend? It was all fake."

"Nothing is fucking fake," I say through clenched teeth. "Either way, it's none of your business."

She looks at me like I've turned orange. "You actually care about her?"

"Yes." She doesn't deserve my answer, but I'm not about to lie about this. "Either way, you shouldn't have meddled in my affairs."

Eidith stares at me with a wounded expression. "But you can do so much better than her."

"Oh?" My voice drips with sarcasm. "Like who?"

"Me," she says and flushes. "Real. Fake. Either way, it would make a lot more sense."

I make sure she can see the disdain on my face as I slowly enunciate, "You and I do *not* make sense. You and I will never happen. Not in a million years. In fact, after today, we will never see each other again."

She staggers back as I add, "Oh, and it goes without saying, but you're fucking fired."

———

For the rest of the day, I try to get a hold of Juno without much success.

The flower delivery guy tells me she tossed the bouquet at his face. She also trashed the chocolates I sent her, and she refused to sign for the jewelry.

The only gift out of many that she accepted was the fairy castle cactus—but she ordered the delivery lady to, and I quote, "Tell the sender that me taking in this poor, overwatered guy doesn't mean squat."

Fine. I just need a more creative way to get her attention.

And I think I have one.

It's crazy, almost fatally so, but I have a feeling that it might just work.

Chapter 39

Juno

I'M MOPING on the couch, rewatching my favorite moment in all of fiction—the scene in *Encanto* when Isabella creates a cactus.

What I'd give for such a power.

Oh, well. I'll have to settle for the cactuses I've got: trusty El Duderino and his new brother, Chateau de Chambord.

Crap. Thinking of the new cactus reminds me of the person who gifted him to me.

Lucius has been extremely persistent over the last three days. There have been calls, voicemails, texts, emails, and various gifts.

If I'm honest with myself, he's beginning to wear me down, but I have to be strong. The thing he most likely wants is to convince me to keep the fake relationship going, and that's not something I—

My phone rings. Is it Lucius again? Is he like the devil—think of him and he calls you?

But no.

It's Pearl, my friend—not Lucius's kinky grandmother.

"Hey," I say, trying not to sound as depressed as I feel. "What's up?"

"I just got a call from your insane billionaire squeeze," she says.

"What?"

"I said I got a call from one Lucius Warren," she says exaggeratingly loudly. "Imagine my surprise."

I jump to my feet. "I don't want to talk to him."

"Yeah. He mentioned that as the reason for reaching out to me. Sounds like you two had a fight—and you didn't tell me a thing about it."

"Sorry. The NDA." In truth, I didn't talk to anyone about Lucius because it's impossible to explain my situation without admitting to all the lies, and I can't bear to get into that.

"Well," she says. "Given the stunt he's about to pull, I think you might want to talk to him."

"Nope. Not happening."

She sighs. "What happened, hon? Was there another woman?"

"No."

She gasps. "Another man?"

"No! He didn't cheat. I don't think he's even interested in... never mind."

There's a silence on her end for a while. Then she says, "Okay. I'm here to talk when you're ready. For now, can you at least tell me how he got my number?"

"No idea. I did mention your name in front of him and his grandmother—because her name is also Pearl. He must have used his billionaire resources to triangulate you."

It might not have even been all that hard. How many young women of our age are named Pearl? Whatever the number, I almost smile picturing Lucius cold-calling all said Pearls and asking them if they have a friend named Juno.

"Okay," she says. "But you'll need to at least talk to him once. Tell him to cancel his dumb idea."

"Which is?"

She tells me.

My eyes go wide and my stomach drops. Then I clench my teeth and demand, "How do I get in touch with him?"

"Check your email," she says. "He said the Zoom video conference is up and running, and that you should have an invite."

"Okay. I'd better go."

"Of course," she says. "But you *will* tell me everything afterward."

"At some point, maybe," I say. "That is, unless you hear about what happened to him on the daily news. 'Billionaire Dies from Idiotic Gesture.'"

"Romantic gesture," she corrects.

Not dignifying that with a reply, I hang up, then grab my computer and locate the email.

Damn.

He's emailed me another dozen times since I last deleted all his messages without reading.

I open the most recent email and click on the link to join the stupid video call.

A second later, there he is, on my screen.

Saguaro give me strength.

Seeing him, I forget everything, including how mad I am and why.

I've missed my stupid human cactus. Missed him so much it hurts.

"Hi," he says from the screen. "Thanks for joining."

I narrow my eyes at him. "It's not like you gave me much choice."

As if to confirm my words, a white Persian cat strolls in front of the camera. Then a Siamese cat. Then one of those bald ones that all the movie villains have jumps onto his shoulder, no doubt thinking herself a parrot to his pirate.

"I wanted to apologize," Lucius says, oblivious to the cat menaces surrounding him. "I wanted to tell you how I feel. In person." He reaches toward the camera and the video cuts off. "A limo is waiting for you. Or if you want to take a cab, the place is called Purrville Cat Cafe."

"Wait!" I shout. "Go outside."

Except it's too late. The call disconnects before he can hear me.

Fuck! Shouldn't a cat cafe check if a patron is allergic to cats before letting him in? Or did he lie to them?

Whatever.

I run for my shoes, glad I was dressed reasonably well when this whole thing started. If he went into anaphylactic shock because I had to change, I don't know what I'd do.

Sprinting outside, I leap into the limo and shout, "Go!"

Elijah must know of Lucius's folly because we get moving at a *Fast and the Furious* pace.

Watching the streets blur, I can't help but picture Lucius's gorgeous features swelling up, his throat closing, and then—

The limo stops.

Whew. At least Purrville Cat Cafe is close enough to my place.

I dash inside, ignoring the front door people saying something about waivers and fees.

Cats are everywhere. It's actually a struggle not to step on a paw or a tail, but I do my best.

When I reach Lucius, he's surrounded by enough cats to give even the most vicious, battle-weary sewer rat nightmares.

"You came," he says, his voice slightly muffled by a fluffy tail wrapped around his face.

I remove the fluffy monster and glare at Lucius's red, swollen eyes. "I refuse to talk here. Outside. Now."

Nodding somewhat gratefully, he stands up and quickly exits Purrville.

As soon as we're on the street, I give him my most seething glower. "Are you out of your mind?"

He shrugs and sneezes violently. "I *had* to see you."

"So you staged a fucking suicide?"

"Nothing so dramatic." He reaches into his pocket and pulls out an EpiPen. "I just needed to show you how serious I was. My life wasn't in danger."

"Bullshit." Still, I sigh in relief, then say with feeling, "You asshole. I was worried." Then, to show him just how much, I push him. Or I intend to.

He captures my wrists and then my gaze. "You were worried about me?"

"Yeah. Obviously. Unlike some, I have human emotions and—"

"I'm sorry." He squeezes my wrists gently. "I didn't mean to worry you."

"Sure you did. And you'd better have a good fucking reason."

"I do," he says solemnly. "I need to tell you something."

The look in his eyes makes me feel light and bubbly all of a sudden—like I might float away, or burst. I fight the feeling because I've been deceived before. Keeping my tone cranky, I say, "Fine. Out with it."

"Okay." He tugs me closer. "I love you."

Or at least, that is what I think I hear him say. It's so shocking that I reply with the dumbest comeback since the times of Ancient Rome: "What?"

He lets go of my wrists to cradle my face in his palms. "I love you, Juno. I need you to know that. I know I don't deserve it, but I want you to date me. For real this time. I hope that over time, you also—"

"I love you too, you idiot!"

"What?" he says, and I don't think he's making fun of my earlier "what?"

I cover his hands with mine. "I said 'you idiot.'"

"Fair," he agrees. "But before that?"

I dampen my lips. "I love you, Lucius. I've been falling for you all this time. I knew it when I realized that you're a cactus. My cactus. Then, when we—"

He silences me in the nicest way possible—with a kiss.

A sweet, gentle one that makes me believe he really means his words—as earth-shattering as they are. Swiftly, the kiss turns R-rated, our tongues mating hungrily as he drops his hands to my hips and pulls me to his aroused body.

And then he pulls away and sneezes. Twice.

I step back and give him a stern onceover.

Yep. He's covered in cat fur, and his eyes are not looking healthy. At all.

"We need to get you out of those clothes," I say. "And into a shower."

His gaze heats up. "Will you join me?"
I pretend to sigh. "If that's what it takes."

Epilogue

Juno

I'm so giddy with excitement I'm worried I'll pee my pants.

It's not just the fact that I'm about to officially become a University of Florida alum. Or that my whole loving family is here for my graduation.

No. The main source of my glee is the man giving away the diplomas up on the stage.

The man who flew said family here on his private jet.

Lucius.

My real, official boyfriend who was asked by the university to perform this honor because he's become a celebrity here in Gainesville due to—among other things—all the jobs the recently finished Novus Rome has created.

Ruefully, I glance down at my outfit—a shapeless black gown.

Not my best. Not when I much prefer wearing sundresses when I see him, with sandals that accentuate my feet—because I know the latter drive him mad.

Then again, maybe this outfit is fine. Maybe having my feet—and everything else—hidden is enticing. Maybe we could incorporate this gown into a bit of roleplay tonight? I could be a naughty Supreme Court justice. Or a—

"Juno Lazko." The words boom ominously over the big speakers.

My mom elbows me in the ribs, in case I've grown deaf.

Jackknifing to my feet, I float to the stage on a cloud of endorphins and adrenaline.

The closer I get to Lucius, the more powerfully my heart flutters.

Our life is about to be different.

Easier.

Nicer.

He's been extremely busy with the project of his dreams and I with my Botany program, and though we've always found time for each other, it's always felt like we we've been stealing that time.

But not after today. Not with the job I have lined up at the Botanical Gardens and his—

"Hey, you," Lucius says to me, covering the microphone. His metallic eyes reflect the bright Florida sun overhead. "Are you excited?"

I nod, beaming.

"Good." He grabs my diploma and steps out from behind the podium, the way he did for the other students. But then he goes off script. Normally, he shakes the graduate's hand at this point, but he doesn't do that to me.

Instead, he drops to one knee—causing everyone gathered to gasp.

In the stunned silence that follows, Lucius pulls out a turquoise-colored box, then clasps my hand in his, looking up at me adoringly—something he has definitely not done with any of the other diploma recipients.

"What is happening?" I whisper down at him.

I mean, obviously I know. I've dreamed of something like this moment. After all, it's been four years.

Still, here of all places? Now?

"Juno," he says, and I'm not sure if it's part of the plan or not, but he's not covering the microphone anymore, so his words ring out across the whole field. "Ever since we got stuck on that elevator together, my life hasn't been the same—and I couldn't be happier." He opens the box, revealing a diamond that reminds me of the one the old lady dropped into the ocean in *Titanic*. "You've been my muse," he continues. "My friend. My everything." He takes out the ring. "Ancient Romans believed that a vein leads directly from the left ring finger straight to the heart—and that belief is the origin of the tradition we're currently participating in."

Of course, leave it to Lucius to tie in Ancient Rome to this proposal.

"So, as I give you your degree, I ask you, Juno Lazko, will you make me the happiest man in the world and marry me?"

I grin so hard my ears hurt. "If I say no, will I still graduate?"

He nods.

"In that case... yes. A thousand times, yes."

As he slides the ring onto my finger and stands up to sweep me into his arms, the entire stadium erupts in cheers—and I realize the Ancient Romans may have been right.

My heart swells with all the blood pumping through the vein leading from my left ring finger. Or more likely, with Lucius's love.

Sneak Peeks

Thank you for participating in Juno and Lucius's journey! If you're eager for more Misha Bell, check out *The Love Deal*!

Looking for more laugh-out-loud romcoms? Meet the Chortsky siblings in *Hard Stuff*:

- *Hard Code* – A geeky workplace romance following quirky QA tester Fanny Pack and her mysterious Russian boss, Vlad Chortsky
- *Hard Ware* – The hilarious story of Bella Chortsky, a sex toy developer, and Dragomir Lamian, a potential investor in her next big business venture
- *Hard Byte* – A fake date romcom featuring Holly, a prime-number-obsessed

Anglophile who makes a deal with Alex Chortsky (a.k.a. the Devil) to save her dream project

For more quirky, irresistibly sweet leading ladies like Juno, try our stories following the Hyman sisters:

- *Royally Tricked* – A raunchy royal romance featuring daredevil prince Tigger and Gia Hyman, a germaphobic, movie-obsessed magician
- *Femme Fatale-ish* – A spy romcom starring aspiring femme fatale Blue Hyman and a sexy (possible) Russian agent
- *Of Octopuses and Men* – An enemies-to-lovers romcom about Olive, an octopus-obsessed marine biologist, and her sizzling hot (and infuriating) new boss
- *Sextuplet and the City* – A laugh-out-loud fake marriage romance about a dessert-loving secret blogger who falls for a hot, Latvian ballet dancer in need of a green card

We love receiving feedback from our readers, and we are always interested to know what you'd like to see in books to come. Want your favorite side character to have their own book? Mention it in a review! We take all suggestions into consideration, and if you sign up for our newsletter at www.mishabell.com, you'll be the first to know who will be featured next!

Misha Bell is a collaboration between husband-and-wife writing team, Dima Zales and Anna Zaires. When they're not making you bust a gut as Misha, Dima writes sci-fi and fantasy, and Anna writes dark and contemporary romance. Check out *Wall Street Titan* by Anna Zaires for more steamy billionaire hotness!

Turn the page to read previews from *Of Octopuses and Men* and *Sextuplet and the City*!

Excerpt from Of Octopuses and Men

By Misha Bell

My grandparents' grumpy neighbor is as hot as the lethal Florida sun. And like the sun, he's bad for me. My taste in men is the worst—just ask my ex and his restraining order.

What am I doing in Florida with my grandparents, you wonder? Well, my best friend is an octopus, and he needs a bigger tank, so I took a job at an aquarium in the Sunshine State.

I didn't expect that sexy, long-haired grump to try to buy my octopus for some nefarious purpose. Nor did I expect to make out with him during a late-night swim at the beach.

And the last thing I expected was to run into him on my first day at my new job... where he's my boss.

———

"Ah, Caper. What are you up to?"

I grin. My name is Olive (my parents are evil in their hippie-dippie-ness), and when Grandpa calls me Caper, he means "little olive," which makes me feel like a little girl again. Obviously, I'll never tell him that his nickname for me is botanically incorrect: capers are the flowers of a shrub, while olives are a tree fruit from an altogether different species.

"Taking Beaky out for a walk," I reply, nodding at the tank.

Grandpa squints at the glass, and Beaky chooses that exact moment to make himself look like a rock—as he does every time Grandpa tries to look at him.

Grandpa rubs his eyes. "Is there really an octopus in there? I feel like you and your grandmother are trying to make me think I'm going senile."

"No. It's Beaky who's messing with you."

I can't blame my grandfather for not spotting my eight-armed friend. When it comes to camouflage, octopuses blow chameleons out of the water. Also, if a chameleon was literally in the water, no amount of camouflage would save it from becoming an octopus's lunch.

Grandpa shakes his head. "Why?"

I shrug. "He's a creature with nine brains, one in his head and one in each arm. Trying to puzzle out his thinking would give anyone a headache."

Grandpa squints at the tank again, but Beaky stays in his rock guise. "Why do you walk him, anyway?"

"To keep him from being bored. What he really needs is a bigger tank, but for now, he'll have to make do with a change of scenery."

"Bored?"

"Oh, yeah. A bored octopus is worse than a seven-year-old boy hopped up on caffeine and birthday cake. In Germany, an octopus named Otto repeatedly shorted out the Sea Star Aquarium's entire electrical system by squirting water at the 2,000-watt overhead spotlight. Because he was bored."

Grandpa lifts his bushy eyebrows. "But don't you make puzzles for him? Let him watch TV?"

I nod. Making puzzles for octopuses is actually what I'm famous for, and how I got my new job. "Toys and TV help," I say, "but I still get the sense he's feeling cooped up."

Grunting, Grandpa delves into his pocket and pulls out a handgun the size of my arm. "Take this with you." He thrusts it at me.

I blink at the instrument of death. "Why?"

"Protection."

"From what? We're in a gated community."

He thrusts the weapon at me with greater urgency. "It's better to have a gun and not need it."

I don't take the offering. "The crime rate in Palm Islet is ten times lower than in New York."

Grandpa takes the clip out of the gun, checks it,

shoves in an extra bullet, and snaps it back in. "It would give me peace of mind if you took it."

"By Cthulhu," I mutter under my breath.

"Bless you," Grandpa says.

"That wasn't a sneeze. I said, 'Cthulhu.'" At Grandpa's blank stare, I heave a sigh. "He's a fictional cosmic entity created by H. P. Lovecraft. Depicted with octopus features."

"Oh. Is that him in your grandmother's sexy cartoons?"

"Absolutely not." I shudder at the thought. "Cthulhu is hundreds of meters tall. He's one of the Great Old Ones, so his attentions would rip a woman apart as quickly as they would drive her mad."

"Fair enough." Grandpa attempts to shove the gun into my hands again. "Take it and go."

I hide my hands behind my back. "I don't have any kind of license."

"You're kidding." He regards me incredulously. "Tomorrow, I'll take you to a concealed carry class."

I fight a Cthulhu-sized eye roll. "I'm kind of busy tomorrow, starting a new job and all."

With a frown, he hides the gun somewhere. "How about this weekend?"

"We'll see," I say as noncommittally as I can before grabbing my handbag from the back of a nearby chair and pressing the remote button again to roll the tank into the garage.

My grandparents, like other Floridians, prefer to leave their houses this way, instead of, say, through the front door.

As soon as my grandfather is out of sight, Beaky stops being a rock, spreads his arms akimbo, and turns an excited shade of red.

"You should be ashamed of yourself," I tell him sternly.

We are the God Emperor of the Tank, ordained by Cthulhu. We shall not bestow the glory of our visage upon the undeserving. Hurry up, our faithful priestess-subject. We want to taste the sunshine on our suckers.

Yup. Ellen DeGeneres talked to a fictional sentient octopus in *Finding Dory*, while my real one speaks to me in my head. And I'm not alone in having these imaginary conversations. Ever since my sisters and I were kids, we've given animals voices. In my mind, Beaky sounds like nine people speaking in unison (the main brain and the eight in his arms), and his tone is imperious (octopuses have blue blood, after all). Oh, and his words come out with that faint gargle-like sound effect used in *Aquaman* when the Atlanteans spoke underwater.

I open the garage door.

It's super bright outside, despite the ancient oaks that provide plenty of shade.

With a sigh, I take a big tube of my favorite mineral-based sunblock from my bag and cover myself with a thick layer from head to foot. The UV index is 10, so I wait a few minutes, and then I cover myself with a second layer. I do this furtively in the garage to avoid my grandparents teasing me about taking a job in the Sunshine State while being paranoid about sun exposure.

And no, I'm not a vampire—though my sister Gia looks suspiciously like she might be, with her goth makeup and all. Avoiding the sun makes legitimate scientific sense given the harmful effects of UV rays, both A and B, as well as blue light, infrared light, and visible light. They all cause DNA damage. This issue got on my radar a couple of years back when Sushi, my pet clownfish, developed skin cancer, probably due to her aquarium being by a window. I've been careful ever since, even going as far as gluing a triple layer of UV-protective coating over Beaky's tank.

Now, do I realize that I worry about the sun a tad more than anyone who isn't a paranoid dermatologist? Sure. But can I stop? Nope. I think some level of neurosis is programed into my DNA, at least if my identical sextuplet sisters are anything to go by. But hey, when I'm in my eighties and look younger than all my sisters, we'll see who has the last laugh.

Sunblocking finished, I throw on a lightweight zip-up jacket that's coated in UV-protective chemicals, a wide-brim hat, and giant sunglasses.

There. If I were really taking this too far, I'd be wearing one of those Darth Vader visors, wouldn't I?

My heartbeat picks up as I follow Beaky's tank out into full sun, but I calm down by reminding myself that the sunblock will do its job. When the tank rolls down the driveway and onto a shady sidewalk by the lake, my breathing evens out further.

So far so good. Now I just hope I don't get too many annoying questions from nosy neighbors.

A pair of herons take flight nearby as we stroll along the lake shore. Beaky stares at them intently and changes his shape a few times.

We wish to taste those things. Be a good priestess-subject and deliver them to the tank.

I pat the top of the tank. "I'll give you a shrimp when we get back."

We both spot a raccoon digging in the grass by the lake, likely looking for turtle or gator eggs.

We wish to taste that too.

"I'll give you a shrimp without the puzzle," I tell him.

Usually, I put his treats into one of my creations, making the meal extra fun for him, but if he's worked up an appetite by watching all the land animals, I don't want to delay his gratification.

A five-foot alligator slowly crawls out of the lake.

Yup, we're definitely in Florida.

Spotting it, Beaky picks up two coconut shells from the bottom of his tank and closes them over his body, appearing to the world—and to the gator—like an innocent coconut.

"That thing can't get you in the tank," I say soothingly. "Not to mention, it's scared of me. Hopefully."

The statistics on alligator attacks are in our favor. In a state with headlines like "Florida man beats up alligator" and "Florida man tosses alligator into Wendy's drive-through window," the gators have learned to stay far, far away from the insane humans.

Because Beaky doesn't read the news or check online statistics, his eye looks skeptical as it peeks out from the coconut shells.

I return my attention to the sidewalk—and spot him.

A man.

And what a man.

He could've starred in *Aquaman* instead of Jason Momoa. If I were casting the leading man for my wet dreams, this guy would definitely get the role.

The thought sends tendrils of heat to my nether regions, specifically the part I privately think of as my wunderpus—in honor of *wunderpus photogenicus*, an amazing octopus species discovered in the eighties.

By the way, I once took a picture of my wunderpus, and it's also *photogenicus*.

But back to the stranger. Strong, masculine features framed by an impeccably trimmed beard, cyan eyes as deep as the ocean, a tanned, muscular body clad in low-riding jeans and a sleeveless top that shows off powerful arms, thick, blond-streaked hair that streams down to his broad shoulders—he'd look like a surfer if it weren't for the broody expression on his face.

Beaky must've forgotten about the gator because he's out of his coconut and looking at the stranger with fascination.

Figures. Aquaman has the power to talk to octopuses, along with other sea creatures.

I realize I'm also gaping at him and tense as he gets closer. Unlike back in New York, where it's customary to pass a stranger without acknowledging their existence, here in Florida, everyone at the very least greets their neighbors.

What do I say if he speaks to me? Do I even dare open my mouth? What if I accidentally ask him to have his way with me?

Wait a second. I think I've got it. He's also walking a pet, in his case a dog of the Dachshund breed, a.k.a. a hotdog dog, the most phallic member of the canine species. All I have to do is say something about his wiener—the one wagging its tail, not his Aquamanhood.

When the man is a dozen feet away, he seems to notice me for the first time. Actually, his gaze zeroes in on Beaky's tank, and his broody expression turns downright hostile—jaw clenched, mouth downturned, eyes flinty. The insane thing is, he looks no less hot now. Maybe more so.

What is wrong with me? No wonder I end up dating assholes like—

His deep, sexy voice is the kind of cold that can create a wind chill even in this humid sauna. "How much for the octopus?"

I blink, then narrow my eyes at the stranger, my hackles rising like spikes on a pufferfish. He wants to buy Beaky? Why? Does he want to eat him?

This *is* the state where people eat gators, turtles (even the protected species), bullfrogs, Burmese pythons, and key lime pie.

Gritting my teeth, I point to the tail-wagging dog at his side. "How much for the bratwurst?"

A sneer twists his full lips. "Let me guess... a New Yorker?"

Aquaman? More like Aqua-ass. "Let *me* guess. Florida man?" I can picture the rest of the headline: "... steals octopus in tank and tries to have sex with it."

Given what my grandmother said about Rule 34 and where I am, it's not that far-fetched. I once read an article about a Florida man who tried to sell a live shark in a mall parking lot. What's sex with an octopus in comparison?

His thick brown eyebrows snap together. "The stories you're alluding to are about transplants. They're never about actual Floridians."

"Oh, I've read what you're talking about," I say with a snort. "'Florida man receives first-ever penis transplant from a horse.' I'm pretty sure the article said that the brave pioneer was born and raised in Melbourne—that's two hours away from here."

Oops. Have I gone too far? Everyone does seem to carry a gun here. And since I found him attractive earlier, with my dating track record, he might well turn out to be dangerous.

Instead of pulling out a weapon, the stranger rubs the bridge of his nose. "Serves me right for trying to argue with a New Yorker. Forget the news. That tank is too small for that octopus. How would you like to live your life inside a Mini Cooper?"

I suck in a breath, my stomach tightening. "How would *you* like to be walked on a leash?" I jerk my chin toward his wiener, whose tail is no longer wagging. "Or to be forced to ignore your screaming bladder and bowels until your master deigns to take you for a walk? Or to have your reproductive organs messed with?"

He glowers at me. "Tofu isn't neutered. In fact, he—"

"Tofu?" My jaw drops. "As in, a tofu hot dog? Talk about animal cruelty."

The veins popping out in his neck look distractingly sexy. "What's wrong with the name Tofu?"

Before I can reply, Tofu whines pitifully.

"Great job," the stranger says. "Now you've upset him."

"I'm pretty sure you did that." *By naming the poor dog Tofu.*

"This conversation is over." He turns his back to me and tugs on the leash. "Come, Tofu."

Tofu gives me a sad look that seems to say, *I don't like it when my daddy and my new mommy argue.*

With a huff, I roll Beaky's tank in the opposite direction.

———

Go to www.mishabell.com to order your copy of *Of Octopuses and Men* today!

Excerpt from Sextuplet and the City

By Misha Bell

What happens in Vegas stays in Vegas. Or does it?

Okay, let me explain. I broke into my crush's dressing room to sniff his tights (not in a pervy way, I swear!) and got busted while, um... you get the idea. He then kind of, sort of blackmailed me into agreeing to a fake green card marriage with him. But hey, I'm not complaining.

Next thing I know, we're on a flight to Vegas to make our friends and family think we had a crazy drunken night and, in the spur of the moment, tied the knot. Except... that's exactly what happens. (Thanks a lot, vodka.)

Considering that he's the most desirable ballet dancer in New York City and I'm a garage-dwelling secret blogger with a major sweet tooth, there's no way this marriage could ever become real. Not to mention my totally crazy family and my aversion to every smell under the sun—except his.

All I can hope for is to not fall in love with my husband. That shouldn't be too hard, right?

———

The ballet I'm watching is *Swan Lake*, and my crush's role is that of Prince Siegfried.

Damn it. I'm jealous of that crossbow he's holding. Given that my goal is to get this man out of my system, seeing him live might've been a step in the wrong direction.

His muscles—especially on his powerful legs—would make a statue of a Greek god weep in envy. His gleaming eyes are pure melted chocolate, and dark chocolate is also what his slicked-back hair reminds me of. His face is angelic, with cheekbones so sharp-edged they look like the hard layer of Crème Brûlée after you break it with a spoon. Oh, but all of that pales in comparison to the bulge in his pants—a feature of so many of my masturbation fantasies that I've even named the contents of it Mr. Big.

So, yeah. Seeing all this is the opposite of helpful—and if I activate the vibrating panties I'm currently wearing, it will make everything that much worse.

Originally, I put on the masturbatory panties because I figured this is my last chance at a ménage à moi with The Russian. If sniffing his tights works as intended, I'll have to resort to some other visual aid for visiting the bat cave—like *Magic Mike*, *300*, or *Charlie and the Chocolate Factory*.

Then again, I shouldn't be selfish. This adventure would make for an amazing blog post. I don't usually get naughty in public, so this might be educational for my followers.

Yeah. I'll do it for them. It will be my last hurrah with The Russian—made that much more interesting because I'm seeing him live.

I scan the nicely dressed people sitting around me. The coast is clear. They're focusing on the spectacle in front of us, as they should.

I fish out the little remote that activates the vibration.

Last chance to change my mind.

Nope. The Russian flashes me the perfection that is his butt, with a gluteus maximus that I want to lick like rock candy.

I press the "on" button and grin as my underwear begins to vibrate.

It's DIY time.

Even at the lowest speed, my clit is instantly engorged, and I have to hope the electrical components inside this technological marvel are waterproof. Soon, I have to painfully bite my tongue to keep from moaning. Tchaikovsky's music is genius, but it wouldn't drown *that* out.

I had no idea it would be this hard to keep quiet. Must be The Russian's hotness in action.

Panting, I turn off the device to give my clit a chance to cool off. If I get caught doing this, I'll be escorted out and banned for life for being the pervert that I am.

When I think I can stay quiet, I turn the thing back on again.

Nope. Just as The Russian performs a particularly mouthwatering *fouetté*, the desire to be vocal is back with a vengeance.

Fuck. Me.

Whoever designed these panties should win some sort of a prize. They do to my nether regions what the Swan theme song does to my ears, or The Russian to my eyes.

An orgasm of cosmic proportions builds inside me, and staying silent takes an effort of will I know I don't possess, so I turn everything off once again, for good this time.

Fucker. Now I'm just really frustrated and cranky.

As if to sharpen my frustration, the ballerina playing Princess Odette shows up.

Can you say "impossible standard of beauty?" Translucently thin on top, she looks like someone who's never tasted a croissant in her life, yet her legs are powerful and seem to go on and on.

I know, I know. My jealousy is as green as a St. Patrick's Day donut. In my defense, her character is supposed to be sweet, noble, and guileless. She, however, dances the part with seduction, like Odile, the evil black swan. Speaking of *Black Swan*, it's all too easy to imagine this woman stabbing someone with a shard of glass, the way Natalie Portman's character did in the movie.

That's it. Decided. Henceforth, this ballerina will be Black Swan in my mind.

As the ballet continues, I cringe each time The Russian touches Black Swan—which is often, especially during the *pas de deux*. In fact, things get so bad that when Princess Odette meets her sad end, I find it hard to empathize.

I'm just glad the show is over. Watching it live was definitely a mistake.

Fighting the exiting crowds, I make my way to the bathroom, where I lock my stall and climb on a toilet to hide my feet as per Blue's instructions for Operation Big Sniff. Her instructions are also why I'm wearing all black—dressy pants appropriate for the venue, a button-up shirt that's slightly too tight on me (I bought it a few pounds ago, so sue me), and a pair of ballet flats that have seen better days but are the fanciest shoes I can run in.

Taking out an earbud, I stick it into my ear and dial Blue.

"Hey, sis," she says. "The crowd is dispersing as we speak. Hold tight."

As I wait, Blue fills me in on all the juicy family gossip, making me wonder how she gathered all this information. No doubt using the same nefarious methods as Big Brother in the dystopian world of *1984*.

"The Latvian Elvis has just left the building," Blue finally says. "And I turned off the cameras in your way, so you can start the op."

"Thanks." I move to hop down from the toilet, but my foot slips and I headbutt the stall door.

Ouch. I see stars in my vision—shaped like urinal cakes.

Worse still, I hear a sploosh.

No! Please no.

Sadly, it's yes.

My phone is swimming in the toilet bowl. Yuck.

"Hey," Blue says in the earbud through crackling static. "Is everything o—"

The rest is an unintelligible hiss.

My poor phone is dead.

I debate fishing it out, as gross as that would be. I've heard you can stick these devices into rice to dry out, and they may resurrect themselves. In the end, I decide against it. The phone is so old it's a stretch to call it "smart." It's better off drowning in the toilet with some dignity, even though I'll have to skip about a hundred trips to Cinnabon to afford a replacement.

The question now is: should I call off the operation?

I no longer have Blue in my ear, but I *have* splurged on this ticket and I don't know when I'll be able to afford another one. Besides, I've gone through all the trouble of learning how to pick a lock, and Blue has done her part already.

All right, I'm going for it.

Taking in a calming breath, I sneak out of the stall.

No one is around.

Good.

As I creep to my destination, I'm glad I memorized the layout of this place instead of relying on the schematics on my phone.

The first lock in my way is easy to pick, and the second door isn't even locked.

When I get to the last corridor, I realize I'm jogging, and by the time I stop next to the door of what should be The Russian's changing room, I'm panting.

Yep. "Artjoms Skulme" is what the tag on the door says. I'm in the right place.

I take out the lockpicks, and the lock yields to my newfound skills without much fuss.

Heart hammering, I step inside. In the large mirror in front of me, I look frightened, like Blue would in a bird's nest. Even my shoulder-length hair appears frazzled and pale, the strawberry-blond of my strands more ashy blond in this light than anything close to red.

Chewing on my lip, I look around for the tights.

I've made it this far, and I'm not leaving without completing the operation.

Hmm.

I don't see tights anywhere.

Just my luck. He's a neat freak.

Wait a sec... I see something. Not tights, but possibly even better. Although also a bit creepier if I think about it too deeply.

I hurry over to the chair on which I've spotted the item—an article of clothing known in this industry as a dance belt.

Except it's not an actual belt.

Designed for ballet dancers with external genitals that can flop about during vigorous jumps, this undergarment looks suspiciously like a thong.

I fan myself.

Just picturing The Russian wearing this butt-floss without tights makes me want to re-enable my vibrating panties.

But no. No time for muffin buttering right now.

I pick up the thong—I mean, dance belt. It feels nice and soft to the touch.

Must be made of boyfriend material.

I peer at the dance belt like I'm trying to charm a snake inside of it. A snake named Mr. Big.

Am I really going to do this? And if I do, does that mean I'm like one of those peeps who buy worn underwear online?

No. I don't have an undies-sniffing fetish, more like the opposite.

Yeah. If anyone asks, that's my excuse.

With determined movements, I rip the filter from each nostril and bring the dance belt up to my nose.

Here goes.

I take the Big Sniff.

————

Go to www.mishabell.com to order your copy of *Sextuplet and the City* today!

About the Author

We love writing humor (often the inappropriate kind), happy endings (both kinds), and characters quirky enough to be called oddballs (because... balls). If you love your romance heavy on the comedy and feel-good vibes, visit www.mishabell.com and sign up for our newsletter.